Utter Contempt.
By: Sarah McCulay

Arcana Intellego.

SARAH MCCULAY

© 2024. Utter Contempt. Edited in the U.S. by Orilsted Publishing Services. Copyright © 2024 Enrique García Guasco. Copyright © 2024 Arcana Intellego / Axioma Editorial S.A. Chile. Hendaya 60, Las Condes, 1353, Metropolitan Region, Chile. All rights reserved. No part of this publication may be reproduced, distributed, or transmitted in any form or by any means, including photocopying, recording, or other electronic or mechanical methods, without the prior written permission of the copyright holder.

For Nicole; even more beautiful than all the diamond of the sea...

"Dies Irae".

Dies iræ, dies illa,
Solvet sæclum in favilla:
Teste David cum Sibylla.
Quantus tremor est futurus,
Quando judex est venturus,
Cuncta stricte discussurus!
Tuba, mirum spargens sonum
Per sepulchra regionum,
Coget omnes ante thronum.
Mors stupebit, et natura,
Cum resurget creatura,
Iudicanti responsura.
Liber scriptus proferetur,
In quo totum continetur,
Unde mundus iudicetur...

The atmosphere in the room is heavy and dark, almost tangible. Shadows stretch across the corners as a faint light barely illuminates the leather armchair where the madman is seated. His posture is relaxed—perhaps too relaxed for what one might expect in a psychiatric consultation. In his hand, he holds a Cuban cigar, from which he exhales leisurely. The dense cloud of smoke rises and disperses through the air, filling it with a strong, lingering aroma. The analyst, uneasy, observes him with disdain but says nothing. Instead, he attempts to steer the conversation, once more, towards something productive.

The analyst fixes him with a steady gaze, his expression serious. Then, with a neutral tone, he poses a question that seems simple but contains a subtle logical trap:

Analyst: —Tell me, is contempt a crime?

The madman keeps the cigar between his fingers, seemingly indifferent as ash falls onto his brown and cream houndstooth wool suit, even onto his white shirt. This gesture, far from careless, has for him an air of nonchalant elegance. He takes his time, unhurried, as though savouring the tension in the air. After a prolonged pause, his response emerges, measured and profound:

Madman: —No, contempt is not a crime. In fact, I would say it is a right, one we should reclaim. Isn't it just to hold in contempt the weak, the abject, the fools? Contempt, far from a fault, is a moral stance, a declaration against that which deserves nothing else.

The analyst takes note, his brow furrowing slightly. The madman's response is as intriguing as it is unsettling, opening the door to a dark terrain of the human psyche.

After a pause, during which the madman cast a kind of despotic gaze, he chose to continue: Contempt is a complex feeling, a blend of disdain and disapproval that skirts hatred, yet never quite reaches it. Where hatred seeks to destroy, contempt merely turns its gaze away, averts its attention, relegates the object to a place of irrelevance.

The madman fixed his gaze intently on his interlocutor and said: From a humanistic perspective, contempt is understood as a defence mechanism; it's a way of protecting one's ideals and values from that which threatens or degrades them.

Contempt can arise when one perceives in another traits or behaviours deemed morally inferior or destructive: cowardice, pettiness, hypocrisy, or ingratitude. It is an emotional response that implies no destructive action, but rather a moral withdrawal, a silent judgement that seeks neither revenge nor correction, simply distance. In feeling contempt, one affirms one's own values by dismissing those of others whom one deems unworthy even of consideration.

The analyst understood that, for the madman, this discourse on contempt was a tool of discernment rather than a drive to amend his own standards. From his perspective, contempt is an inherent right, an expression of individual freedom, a conscious choice of whom to respect and whom to disregard, unbound by moral impositions. In this sense, the madman claims contempt not as an act of malice but as a dignified stance in the face of mediocrity or depravity.

The analyst scribbled something in his notepad. Without concealing his distaste, he scrutinises the madman closely. His tone hardens; he wants to guide the man towards deeper introspection, or perhaps towards a contradiction. Then, he poses a direct, cutting question:

Analyst: —Do you reckon it's right to hold others in contempt?

The madman offers the faintest of smiles, and a glint of defiance sparks in his gaze. He takes a final draw on his cigar and, after a measured pause, responds with a blend of irony and conviction:

Madman: —"Believing" doesn't have much to do with "thinking," wouldn't you agree? I assumed that coming here didn't bind me to any act of faith, but rather to an exercise in reflection. But, if what you're after is some sort of contrition, then yes, I'll say that I "believe" contempt is perfectly acceptable.

The analyst jots this down, and the madman catches the subtle movement of his pen against paper. Then, with a slower, deeper tone, he continues, as if explaining something self-evident:

Madman: —In truth, I think what you're really trying to get at is the measure of anger that contempt might contain. Allow me to clarify: what you want to understand is the limit of contempt. If you consider it, we all despise someone or something, and, indeed, we despise certain aspects of ourselves. We don't scold ourselves for it, do we? We do it almost as an involuntary act.

The analyst appears momentarily intrigued. This new perspective that the madman proposes turns contempt into something inherent, almost natural—a human response, hard to dismiss or condemn. The room returns to a heavy silence, as the two of them engage in a subtle duel of thoughts.

The analyst, scribbling haphazardly, attempts to express that, for the madman, contempt could be seen as an emotion that doesn't seek to destroy but rather to define distance.

For the madman, contempt isn't a negative or impulsive emotion; it's a conscious stance, a personal affirmation. He defends it as a right that society silently practises: we despise others, and occasionally, we despise ourselves. By casting it as something "involuntary," the madman suggests that this feeling is, at its core, an intrinsic part of the human experience—inevitable and perhaps necessary to understand who we are and who we wish not to be.

The tension in the room intensifies; the air is thick, almost oppressive. Noticing the analyst's discomfort, the madman decides to seize control of the conversation. With theatrical flair, he extends his right hand towards the analyst's face, stopping just short of touching him, but with a proximity that underscores his sense of superiority. His voice becomes firm, almost entrancing, as he watches his interlocutor's reaction.

Madman: —Anger, doctor, is the very engine that drives human behaviour. That's why the act of exercising violence is so meaningful; it's not just the violence itself, but how active it is, and who wields it. —He pauses, with a slight smirk—. Though, naturally, to grasp this, you'd have to be a barrister, and a fine one at that.

The analyst remains silent, visibly unsettled yet attentive. The madman continues, his tone now more measured, like someone unfolding a carefully prepared lesson.

Madman: —Contempt, on the other hand, can be something as simple as an expression of distance, a lack of interest. It doesn't always imply violence, but it can still inflict pain on the one who becomes its target, for to be despicable is, in a way, to be abominable. Contempt, doctor, kills slowly; it segregates, it marginalises, it doesn't deliver the final blow, but it uses every tool to make sure the despised understands and accepts their status.

The analyst's expression shifts; the distaste on his face is clear, and in an unprofessional lapse, he responds, almost muttering through clenched teeth:

Analyst: —Believe me, I understand perfectly well the concepts of violence and anger.

The madman lets out a short, satisfied laugh. His voice softens, though his tone is unmistakable, brimming with irony and a peculiar kind of compassion.

Madman: —Then you've grasped not only violence, but contempt itself. Because contempt, dear doctor, is also a form of violence. And it seems you've already felt its edge.

Contempt, as the madman suggests, is a subtle form of violence—a form of aggression that doesn't strike outright but marginalises and distances, provoking an emotional erosion that intensifies over time, often leaving no way back. From a psychological angle, contempt can deliver a profound wound to the self-esteem of the person subjected to it, as they are treated as unworthy, irrelevant, or loathsome. It's not physical violence, but a silent rejection that impacts one's self-perception and sense of belonging.

The madman's reflections on "anger" and "violence" reveal a provocative view, in which both emotions are seen as forces inherent to the human condition. Violence, as he sees it, has shades and degrees, with contempt being its most passive manifestation—an act requiring no physical action but still causing harm and destruction through indifference or silent judgement.

To the madman, contempt is not a simple act of rejection; it's a tool for maintaining distance, a way to draw boundaries against that which is deemed unworthy. The goal isn't to end the other with a single blow, but to allow them to sink into their own insignificance and misery. In this sense, contempt can be seen as a mechanism of power, a way to exert influence without acting, to inflict harm without lifting a finger.

The analyst decides to change his approach. Perhaps, he thinks, if he appeals to the madman's ego, acknowledges his intelligence, he might gain his trust and coax him into letting down his guard. So, with a soft voice, almost condescending, he tries a bit of flattery:

Analyst: —It's clear you're an intelligent man...

But the madman cuts him off immediately, his face twisting into a look of distaste, and his tone takes on a cold, almost cutting edge.

Madman: —Don't flatter me, doctor. I'm an old man and strong enough not to tolerate such nonsense. —He pauses, with a smile that seems to hold a bitter mockery—. When I was young, I had an ugly wife, and later she grew fat —he chuckles briefly, relishing the analyst's discomfort—. Look, doctor, the ugliness I could forgive; the fat, however, I found abominable.

The analyst holds back a reaction of surprise, but the madman continues, now with a calculated seriousness, like a judge passing down a sentence.

Madman: —I see much the same in you now: I've realised you're not particularly clever, but I cannot allow you to flatter me. The first is regrettable, yes, but the second, doctor, is unforgivable.

Silence once again fills the room. The rawness of the madman's words has left the analyst without an immediate reply, and the madman watches him with a blend of pity and satisfaction, delighting in his discomfort. It's as though the dialogue has shifted from a conversation to a game of chess, where each word, each gesture, is a calculated move.

The madman's disdain for flattery reveals a rejection of any form of hypocrisy. In his view, being falsely or manipulatively complimented is a greater affront than a lack of intelligence itself. To him, flattery represents a violation of authenticity; he sees accepting both one's own and others' flaws as preferable to covering them up with lies or false praise.

His mention of his young wife shows how the madman views certain human traits as more or less tolerable according to his own value system, which is rooted in a brutal sincerity of flaws. By forgiving her ugliness but abhorring her weight, he implies that some aspects seem inevitable or intrinsic, while others, like flattery or appearance, are personal choices he refuses to tolerate.

In this power play with the analyst, the madman sets the rules: respect can only exist where there's authenticity. Flattery, therefore, isn't just unnecessary to him; he sees it as an attempt at manipulation, something unforgivable that, in his view, resembles an insult wrapped in a compliment. To the madman, any attempt at empty or feigned praise is a show of disrespect towards his strength and intellect—even if that intellect is as dark as the room in which they both sit.

The analyst, surprised and somewhat unsettled, merely raises his eyebrows, observing the madman in silence. Across from him, the madman calmly finishes his cigar, allowing the last tendrils of smoke to dissipate into the room. After a calculated pause, he reaches into the inner pocket of his coat and pulls out a small, conical tin, opening it deliberately. Inside, there's a fresh cigar, which he holds up to the analyst with a nearly defiant gesture.

Madman: —Does it bother you, doctor?

The analyst sighs, realising the madman has him caught in yet another twisted game. With barely concealed irritation, he replies:

Analyst: —Do you even care if it bothers me?

The madman's smile glints with a faint air of superiority. He sighs as he opens the absurd little tin, positioning the cigar between his fingers. His voice is cold, stripped of any hint of warmth.

Madman: —No, I don't, really. It's just a simple courtesy… And you, doctor, were supposed to answer, "No, not at all." Then, I'd have gone ahead and done as I pleased, and you'd have felt satisfied, thinking you had some say in it. In the end, I'd have got my way, as I always do. Now, though, I could still do as I please, but that would be… awkward.

A dense, even more uncomfortable silence takes hold of the room. The madman studies the analyst, seemingly savouring the disorientation his words have stirred up. Finally, without giving the situation another thought, he takes the cigar, lights it with a measured determination, and exhales the first wisp of smoke, regarding him coolly.

Madman: —All right then, doctor. I'll give you a bit of what you really want.

The statement hangs in the air, loaded with ambiguity. What exactly is it that the analyst wants? Answers? Provocation? A final showdown? The madman seems to know, and his expression reflects a mixture of defiance and a hint of pity, as if he's on the verge of revealing something dark and unsettling.

The dialogue between the madman and the analyst morphs into a power game, where courtesy is merely a façade for the madman's assertion of his will. To him, the so-called "act of courtesy" isn't genuine; it's simply a tactic to make the analyst play by his rules. By proposing a choice that offers the analyst no real freedom, the madman illustrates how courtesy, when twisted, can become a tool of control. The choice he grants the analyst is illusory: the analyst never truly had any influence over the madman's behaviour.

In doing so, the madman reveals an underlying truth about human interactions: gestures of kindness or consideration are often strategies to assert one's own will, while the other is led to believe they hold some sway or influence. Here, the madman underscores that he holds the control and can, at any moment, do as he pleases, manipulating the situation to show the analyst he's at his mercy. That final response—offering "a bit of what you really want"—suggests the madman sees the analyst's hidden motives and is prepared to expose them, maintaining absolute dominance over the encounter.

The madman fixes his gaze on the analyst, exhaling a final cloud of smoke. In a calm, almost didactic tone, he begins to unfold his theory on anger, as though revealing a fundamental principle of human nature.

Madman: —Anger, doctor, begins where the territory of all that we don't control begins. To master the world, you've got to first master yourself, have a plan. Isn't that the root of it all? Isn't that what makes us human?

He pauses, letting his words linger in the air. His gaze hardens as he continues.

Madman: —Anger, when it spills over, rules the weak-spirited. A day comes when you're no longer the one in control of it; it controls you. You become its governed, its servant, without even knowing where it comes from, how it seeps into you. But you do its bidding without question. People kill each other, doctor, because they don't know how to control themselves.

The analyst listens, motionless, his dark eyes fixed on the madman, who resumes his cigar and continues, now with a tone darker, laden with intrigue.

Madman: —If you want to control someone, wield disdain over them. Doesn't matter who they are; disdain is a powerful weapon.

Want someone to pull away from you? Show disdain. Want them closer? Show even more disdain. Because the level of disdain dictates the intensity of the reaction, and in the complexity of human nature, the outcome is always the same.

The madman leans back in his chair, satisfied with his words, while the analyst sits still, barely containing an emotion that begins to flicker across his face. Then, suddenly, without warning, the analyst drops his notebook, letting it fall to the floor with a sharp thud. His response escapes him almost involuntarily, brimming with fury.

Analyst: —Rubbish!

The echo of his outburst rings through the room. For a moment, they both sit in silence, the madman's eyes gleaming with a mix of amusement and challenge. The analyst, aware of his own eruption, closes his eyes and takes a deep breath, trying to regain his composure. He forces himself back into control, straightening up in his seat and attempting to steer the conversation back on track, though both know something's fractured in his professional façade.

The madman's theory on anger and contempt reveals a deeply calculated view of human psychology. From his perspective, anger is the price of lacking control, a force that consumes those who haven't mastered their own impulses. To him, the ability to rule oneself is the bedrock of human existence; those who give in to anger become enslaved by it, governed without even realising their submission.

Contempt, on the other hand, emerges in his discourse as an instrument of power, a tool of manipulation that needs neither shouting nor blows. By showing contempt, the madman suggests one can influence another's will, whether to drive them away or draw them close. The intensity of contempt, he claims, elicits a predictable and universal reaction, no matter the personality of the one receiving it. To the madman, this act of contempt is a tool of control, a way to play with another's will, a means of asserting superiority without physical exertion, relying instead on a psychological manipulation he believes foolproof.

The analyst's reaction—momentarily losing control at hearing these theories—demonstrates how contempt can indeed be a trigger for emotions. In his outburst, he expresses not only disagreement but an indignation that shatters his professional role. The analyst's eruption suggests that the madman's speech has penetrated an emotional barrier, proving that, just as the madman predicted, contempt and control can activate instinctive and complex responses in the human mind.

The madman takes a moment to breathe deeply, as if savouring the tension-laden air in the room. Slowly, he rests his cigar on the edge of the small round table beside him, his movements deliberately calculated, as if staging a theatrical scene. With an almost paternal expression, he leans forward, resting his elbows on his knees, and fixes his gaze on the analyst, watching him with an intensity that borders on defiance.

Madman: —You may not agree with me, doctor —he says in a calm, measured voice—. But the fact you don't share my view doesn't make me wrong. —He pauses for a moment, his eyes boring into the analyst's—. After all, I'm twice your age, and I've racked up a fair bit more experience in life...

The madman pauses, as if what he's about to say matters less than what he's about to ask. With calculated subtlety, he drops a question that cuts like a dagger:

Madman: —Tell me, doctor... was it your dad or your mum?

The question catches the analyst completely off guard. His expression betrays him: his eyebrows shoot up, his lips part, and a shadow of surprise crosses his face. He finds no immediate words, and when he tries to respond, all he manages is a stammer. It's clear the question has struck a raw nerve. He tries to shift the subject, awkwardly dodging the conversation with unusual clumsiness.

The madman watches in silence, noting the analyst's discomfort, but decides not to push him further. Instead of forcing him to the brink, he pauses, and in a tone that's both understanding and tinged with irony, he adds:

Madman: —Don't worry, doctor. I'm not the analyst here, but let's just say I know enough to understand a few things. —The insinuation hangs in the air, enough to provoke a reaction in the analyst without pushing him beyond his own defences.

SILENCE FILLS THE ROOM once again, but this time it's tinged with something different, a sense of vulnerability that the analyst tries to reclaim, while the madman watches him with a mix of triumph and compassion, as if he's taught him a lesson without uttering a word.

The madman's display shows that his experience allows him to see straight through his interlocutor's defences and mechanisms. He knows his question will unsettle the analyst, and rather than pressing the point, he withdraws strategically, leaving the analyst with the sense that he, too, is a subject under scrutiny. This not only enables him to keep control of the conversation but also projects an image of wisdom and authority, reinforcing his position of power in the dialogue.

To the madman, the ability to observe and detect emotional weaknesses in others is a skill acquired and honed over the years. His final phrase, "I know enough to understand certain things," serves as a hint of his mastery in the art of understanding and manipulating the human condition, momentarily turning the analyst into the true subject of their conversation.

In an act of defiance, the analyst fires off the question he'd been saving until the end, his tone cutting and direct:

Analyst: —Was it you who killed Kurt Kendall?

The madman goes still for a moment, then a smile of relief spreads across his face, as though he's finally been freed from an endless wait.

Madman: —Ah, at last... I thought you'd never ask. —His tone is almost patient, as if he's willing to offer an explanation, while carefully sidestepping any definitive answer—. You know, you've taken the longest to pose that question to me. And the funny thing is, I've quite enjoyed your approach to contempt. But I do find it curious that you've jumped so quickly from contempt to murder. From where I stand, those two notions are hardly compatible, at least in the semantic sense.

He pauses, looking at him intently, and continues with a tone that almost suggests a confession, though its ambiguity is disconcerting.

Madman: —Though... I must admit, I now feel morally obliged to give you an answer. It seems I've struck a nerve in you, which means that contempt has served its purpose, wouldn't you agree? But as for killing... Blood gives me a bit of disgust, to be honest. Ever since I was a child, I couldn't stand getting messy, not even with food. It's not that I fear blood, no, but culturally, I can't tolerate even the thought of eating offal, even if it's properly cooked. I see it as a sign of moral and intellectual inferiority.

The analyst listens carefully, trying to decipher if there's any hidden clue in his words. The madman carries on, with an almost unsettling calm.

Madman: —Every time I get asked this question, whether I killed Mr Kendall, I have to say no. Because, instantly, my mind conjures up an image of myself stabbing him in the gut, watching as the intestines, the gallbladder, the liver all spill out, my hands drenched in blood. And I've always been... far too weak to do something like that myself.

He pauses, as if savouring the analyst's bewilderment, then concludes in a reflective tone:

Madman: —So no, I didn't kill him. But if the question were, "Did you drive him to take his own life?" then perhaps my answer might be different. However, that's something only you could determine in an interview with him... and since he's dead, it seems we'll have to construct a theory to satisfy both your curiosity and the prosecutor's.

The room falls into silence, laden with a tension that's almost tangible. The madman's answer is ambiguous, sowing doubt without confirming it, slipping through words with a skill that leaves the analyst baffled. It's as though he's toying with him, leaving a suspicion hanging in the air without offering a shred of truth.

In this response, the madman showcases a masterful technique of ambiguity and manipulation. On one hand, he admits his aversion to blood and his scruples against physical violence; on the other, he hints that contempt and mental manipulation could push someone toward self-destruction. By suggesting he might have "driven" Kurt Kendall to suicide, he implies an indirect responsibility, a form of violence he considers subtler and, in a way, morally more acceptable.

His detailed account of disgust towards blood, innards, and the act of "getting dirty" is not just an attempt to project revulsion for the physical act of killing but also a means to control the analyst's perception. He presents his repugnance as a barrier that would prevent him from committing a direct murder, while subtly planting the notion that his disdain may well have done the job.

The madman takes on a grandiose stance, as though imparting some universal lesson, and speaks with calculated emphasis:

Madman: —Mr Kendall was a weak man... —The word "weak" seems to carry a particular weight in his mouth, as if he savours each syllable before letting it drop into the air—. Weakness, doctor, has everything to do with how one approaches life, with the inability to face it with the strength it demands.

The analyst watches the madman, his face etched with scepticism, and fires back a direct, almost accusatory objection:

Analyst: —But you isolated him, you cut him off from everyone.

The madman smiles, a mix of sarcasm and amusement flickering across his face, as if he finds some naivety in the analyst's statement.

Madman: —I thought we were talking about a person, not an electrical cable.

His comment lands in the room with a mocking tone, underscoring his disdain for the analyst's simplistic interpretation. To him, the idea of "isolating" a person suggests a lack of autonomy, a dependency he holds in utter contempt. In his view, Kendall's weakness was his own responsibility, a reflection of his inability to stand alone without the support of others. By reducing the concept of "isolation" to a mere metaphor of an "electrical cable," the madman minimises his role in the situation, turning a serious accusation into a taunt.

The madman uses the word "weak" as an absolute judgement on Kendall's character, drawing a dividing line between those who can face life with strength and those who, as he implies, need to lean on others. This rigid definition of weakness allows him to justify his disdain and even his possible manipulation of Kendall, for to the madman, being weak is practically a moral flaw, a lack of worth that Kendall was forced to bear.

When the analyst points out that he "isolated" Kendall, the madman derails the conversation with sarcasm, taking the word literally and comparing Kendall to an inanimate object. In doing so, he distances himself from any responsibility in Kendall's emotional decline, while also revealing his own contemptuous view: for him, relying on others is a sign of inferiority, a weakness worthy of disdain and, ultimately, a path to self-destruction.

The madman maintains his defiant stance, his tone taking on an almost philosophical air as he justifies his role in Kendall's story. His words, though they seem rational, are laced with a chilling emotional detachment.

Madman: "Doctor, I couldn't have isolated a person if they truly deserved that title. It'd be utterly impossible. Us humans don't wield nearly enough influence over others' realities to dictate choices of such magnitude, let alone one as drastic as the one you're suggesting."

He pauses, letting his words linger in the air, then adds with a steady, calculating gaze:

Madman: "Might I remind you, a court in London determined my innocence."

The analyst, observant, senses the madman leaning on the court's verdict as a shield against any moral judgement. In this reply, the madman seems to emphasise the idea that each individual is ultimately responsible for their own decisions and that no one, however manipulative, has the power to influence another to such an irreversible end. It's an argument that shrinks his responsibility while hinting at a dismissive indifference toward those he sees as emotionally dependent or vulnerable, like Kendall.

The madman's response constructs a defence based on individual autonomy. By suggesting that no one can influence another to the point of a drastic decision, he sidesteps any moral or emotional accountability. To him, those who are "influenced" to the extent of losing control over their actions lack the strength needed to be fully human in his estimation of what it means to "deserve to be" a person.

The reference to the London court is yet another manipulation tactic: he invokes a legal judgement as proof of innocence, though he knows that morality and legality don't always align. In his logic, having been absolved by the judicial system, any further questioning is needless and, to his mind, unfair. With this statement, he places himself above moral or emotional scrutiny, emphasising once more his belief that strength and self-control are the true markers of humanity and dignity.

The analyst, aware that the madman is steering the conversation, decides to regain control. His voice is firm and direct:

Analyst: "Could you describe to me how you met Mr Kendall?"

The madman, unhurried, takes one last drag of his cigar, settles back in his chair, and after a brief pause, begins to recount, as though about to tell a trivial story.

Madman: "It was an autumn afternoon. I remember the sun had a golden hue... though, honestly, it might've been overcast. I'm not entirely certain."

The analyst, observing every movement and gesture, knows the madman is feigning. He suspects that, in truth, the madman recalls every detail of that moment but cloaks it in vagueness to keep control.

Madman: "I met Mr Kendall through Stephany McBride, the daughter of an old friend from Oxford." He pauses, a slight smile appearing on his face, as if he's relishing an ironic pleasure in his own memories. "Linda, Stephany's mother, always struck me as a foolish woman, a bit mad... though not in the good way, like me," he says, gesturing to himself with an air of superiority, as though his own "madness" were a refined trait. His smile widens. "And the daughter, that's Stephany, was even more foolish than her mother."

The madman seems to revel in the details, and with a look of disdain, he adds:

Madman: "The best part was that she had these ridiculous fleurs-de-lis tattooed on the backs of her ankles, like something off a Breton banner. You see, doctor, I've always paid attention to the most minute details. It's undoubtedly a sign of masochism."

The analyst raises an eyebrow, intrigued and slightly puzzled by the connection, and asks sceptically:

Analyst: "And why are you so certain Miss McBride's a masochist?"

The madman looks at him with an expression of utter superiority, as though explaining the obvious to someone who lacks basic understanding.

Madman: "Because, doctor, no one in their right mind tattoos something so ghastly on such a sensitive spot."

The madman's response is both intriguing and disdainful, a thinly veiled critique that seems to reveal far more about himself than about Stephany. The analyst, aware of the apparent triviality of his words, recognises that within this disdain lies a particular scorn for those he deems inferior or incapable of comprehending the depth of his own actions.

By this point, the madman reveals a side of himself that uses both contempt and an obsessive attention to detail as tools of control and superiority. Recalling Stephany and her mother, he makes degrading comments, highlighting what he sees as their "stupidity," reducing their worth as individuals to a few physical traits or tastes he finds absurd. His criticism of Stephany's tattoo isn't just about the design; it's an observation he interprets as evidence of poor judgement and, therefore, inferiority.

To the madman, insignificant details —like the type of tattoo and its placement— are clues that reveal a person's character. This fixation on the trivial, which he presents as a special skill, bolsters his sense of superiority by suggesting that he notices and understands what others overlook. His "attention to the tiniest details" becomes another way of expressing his disdain for those who fall short of his standards of intelligence or taste, creating an unbridgeable gulf between himself and others.

His description of the tattoo as "masochism" is a judgement that projects his own values and prejudices, constructing an emotional and social barrier that allows him to despise those he sees as unworthy, while simultaneously reinforcing his own sense of control and dominance in his conversation with the analyst.

The madman reclines in his chair, smoking his cigar with an air of satisfaction as he continues his story.

Madman: "As I was saying, that afternoon Miss McBride arranged a meeting between Mr Kendall and myself at some old bar. It was one of those places I used to frequent in my youth, back when I hadn't yet acquired too many convictions. Deep down, I thought it was a dreadful idea, but my friendship with her mother left me feeling obliged to attend. I'd planned to have a couple of scotches, get up from the table, and fulfil my duty with minimal effort."

He pauses, regarding the analyst with an almost sneering smile before going on:

Madman: "But when I met Mr Kendall, he struck me as… tepid, a man without character. Frankly, he reminded me of a striped sock; one of those people you might spot shuffling around Piccadilly Circus, insignificant and weak, without a shred of talent."

The analyst interrupts, intrigued and slightly irritated by the madman's condescending tone.

Analyst: "And what do you mean by talent? What should a person have to be worthy of that 'talent'?"

The madman lets out a small laugh, as though the question strikes him as naïve. Leaning forward, his cold, calculating gaze fixes on the analyst.

Madman: "Doctor, talent is what makes a person worth noticing, listening to, taking seriously. It's what separates those living insignificant lives from those capable of affecting the world around them. Talent is the ability to mould reality, to impose one's own will. A talented man doesn't get swept along by the current; he challenges it, reshapes it."

He pauses, savouring the impact of his words, then concludes in an almost theatrical tone:

Madman: "Mr Kendall had none of that. He was a man who, in the end, represented nothing. He had neither character nor purpose, and certainly not the ability to transcend his own mundane existence."

The analyst listens in silence, sensing that the madman defines talent not as a particular skill but as a force of will, a capacity for control and manipulation that, in his view, justifies existence. For him, this concept of talent serves as a measure of worth, a justification for his contempt towards those who don't meet his standards.

To the madman, "talent" isn't a specific ability or an achievement to be displayed, but rather an expression of power and control, an ability to impose one's will upon others and the world. This definition reflects his view of life as a competition where only those who stand out, who influence and manipulate, deserve respect or consideration.

By labelling Kendall as "lukewarm" and "talentless," the madman sets a moral and social hierarchy in which he places himself above those lacking "talent." Through this concept, he justifies his disdain and possibly his treatment of people like Kendall, considering them unworthy of his respect or even his empathy.

The madman's notion of talent as a synonym for dominance and defiance of the norm underscores his disdain for mediocrity and the ordinary. It reveals a psyche that constantly seeks to distinguish and affirm itself as exceptional.

The madman continues his account, as if distancing himself from the experience he describes, speaking with an almost indifferent calm.

Madman: "Mr. Kendall approached me and asked for my advice… as a strategist. He wanted me to help him manage a hefty sum he'd be receiving from the State."

The analyst interrupts immediately, his curiosity piqued by this detail.

Analyst: "From the State?"

Madman: "Yes, that's what Mr. Kendall said," the madman replies with a barely perceptible smirk. "At least, that's what he claimed."

He pauses, carefully stubbing out the remainder of his cigar in the ashtray, and with almost ceremonial movements, reaches into his jacket's inner pocket for a mint. He unwraps it without touching it directly, then pops it into his mouth with a crunch that echoes in the room, catching the analyst's attention. Then, without warning, the madman extends his hand to the analyst, almost forcing him to take another mint.

Madman: "The trouble with smoking, doctor, is it leaves you with bad breath."

The analyst remains still for a moment, surprised by the madman's imposing gesture, but takes the mint without a word. The madman, satisfied, reclines once more in his chair, a mocking smile creeping onto his lips as he resumes his story.

Madman: "In the end, Kendall managed to convince me to be his strategy advisor. He was over the moon when I said I'd take it on..." He laughs, a harsh sound laced with irony and satisfaction. "Poor man; he almost made me feel sorry for him."

The madman watches the analyst, waiting for his reaction as he savours the mint like someone savouring a memory. In his laughter and calculated gestures, the madman exudes a blend of superiority and contempt towards Kendall, portraying him as a weak man who, in his view, made the mistake of seeking guidance from someone he deemed infinitely superior.

The madman deploys a series of gestures and words that suggest both disdain and a subtle but unmistakable display of control over the analyst. By forcefully offering the mint, he imposes his will in a small but significant act. The unspoken message is that, even in a trivial gesture, he decides, and the analyst merely complies, reflecting how the madman delights in projecting his dominance even in the most minor details.

The story of his advising Kendall adds another layer to his scorn. The madman describes Kendall's enthusiasm with a derisive laugh, as though merely having someone like him agree to help was an extraordinary concession, something that, in his mind, should have provoked an overblown reaction from the man. To the madman, Kendall's interest in his advice confirms his dependency and weakness, further reinforcing his sense of superiority over those he deems inferior.

In his recounting, the madman not only expresses his contempt for Kendall but also uses every detail — the mint gesture, the ironic retort, the derisive laughter — as tools to reaffirm his sense of control, both in his relationship with Kendall and in his present interaction with the analyst.

The analyst, keeping his tone incisive, asks a direct question:

Analyst: "So, you... were supposed to tell him how to defraud the State?"

The madman cuts him off at once, with a barely concealed look of irritation.

Madman: "I don't have to answer that!"

The analyst, sensing he's hit a nerve, offers a calculatedly neutral apology and rephrases the question, attempting not to provoke another negative reaction.

Analyst: —My apologies. Let me rephrase: in what exactly would you be advising Mr. Kendall?

The madman remains silent for a few moments, scrutinising the analyst with a mix of disdain and calculation, as if deciding just how much he wants to reveal of his game. Finally, he replies with a calm, measured voice.

Madman: —Essentially, doctor, I'd make him trust himself. Though that's what someone like you would do. Me, I'd merely make him feel... real.

The analyst furrows his brow, intrigued, on the verge of probing further. But the madman continues, pre-empting the question, his tone laced with an almost cryptic irony.

Madman: —Do you understand, doctor? Weak people like Kendall need more than just confidence; they need a reason to believe they're real people, something that confirms their existence. So, rather than "teaching" him anything, I'd help him build the illusion that his decisions matter. Nothing is more powerful for a man without character than the feeling of being taken seriously.

The analyst watches in silence, perceiving the cold detachment with which the madman exploits the insecurities of others. For the madman, "advising" was never about practical or moral guidance; it was an act of power: he provided Kendall with a hollow sense of worth and purpose, without actually transforming him in any meaningful way.

The madman redefines "advice" in a profoundly manipulative manner. Rather than genuinely helping Kendall improve his confidence or skills, his intent was to make Kendall believe his life had some kind of value, even if it was all an illusion. This distinction reveals a calculated purpose: he didn't view Kendall as an equal, but as a weak figure he could shape to his convenience.

To the madman, "weak" people like Kendall are undeserving of real change; instead, they merit only a shallow imitation of confidence, a constructed reality that gives them a fleeting sense of importance. This, in his eyes, is the "talent" of a manipulator: creating the illusion of value in someone who, by his judgement, lacks it.

Through his response, the madman presents himself as someone who, rather than improving others' lives, sees himself as the sole arbiter of what is "real" for others, reinforcing his sense of superiority and control over those he deems inferior.

The analyst, undeterred by the madman's challenging attitude, presses further, intent on prising more details from him.

Analyst: —So, you'd make Mr. Kendall feel "real." And how exactly would you do that?

The madman, without missing a beat, responds in a sharp, slightly mocking tone:

Madman: —Professional secret, doctor. If I gave away my methods to anyone lounging in a fancy leather chair, I wouldn't be here sitting with you.

He pauses, relishing the confusion his words have stirred, and with an ironic smile, he adds:

Madman: —In fact, I'd probably have moved to Bengal with some old mate. Become a hunter. Though, naturally, I wouldn't have had the cash for those fine cigars I'm so fond of.

The madman reclines in his chair, observing the analyst with a look of smug satisfaction. His answer not only dodges the question but turns the conversation into a battle of wits, making it clear that he doesn't see himself as someone who can be easily unravelled. For him, his "methods" are a secret art, something that defines him and that he alone controls.

The analyst sits in silence, sensing that the madman has no intention of providing concrete answers. Instead, he has used the question as an opportunity to bolster his image as someone exceptional, someone who, in his own mind, lies beyond any professional or moral examination.

The madman's evasion of the analyst's question is a clear demonstration of how he uses the notion of "professional secret" to craft an aura of mystery and power. Instead of disclosing his "method" for manipulating people like Kendall, the madman indulges in a fantasy of an alternative lifestyle —the hunter in Bengal— that underscores his self-perception as a unique being, for whom methods of control and manipulation are both natural and reserved for him alone.

The reference to cigars reinforces this image, suggesting that, in his hierarchy of values, controlling others is as much a luxury as a personal necessity. For the madman, this evasive manoeuvre not only sidesteps a direct answer but redirects the conversation, making it clear that his power over Kendall (and, in this moment, over the analyst himself) is something he considers unreachable and incomprehensible to others.

In essence, the madman doesn't just dodge the question—he flips it into a declaration of superiority: he hints that his methods are an arcane art, reserved only for those who can grasp and wield them, a skill he sees as unique to himself, elevating him beyond any moral scrutiny or judgement.

The madman, reclining back with a look of smug satisfaction, seems intent on distilling his theory for the analyst. His tone drips with condescension, as though he's unveiling an obvious truth everyone else stubbornly chooses to ignore.

Madman: —Let me put it simply, doctor. If you look at why a man is taken seriously —in Parliament, at the palace, wherever— it all boils down to a bit of showmanship, doesn't it? A bit of theatre, a façade. It's the manners, doctor, that make people think a man's born with a silver spoon or grew up in Notting Hill.

He pauses, letting his words sink in, then carries on, his tone slower, almost as if he's giving a lesson:

Madman: —Those manners are what convince us someone's worth paying attention to. But truth is, no one really knows a thing; they're all running on impressions—believing whatever someone else's manners make them believe. And first impressions are nearly always linguistic: how someone speaks, how they enunciate.

The analyst listens, realising that for the madman, authenticity is a mere illusion, crafted to get what one wants. In his view, a person's "worth" is nothing more than an act, and those who succeed are simply adept at maintaining that façade. For him, a person's true essence is irrelevant; what matters is mastering these "manners," for it's through them that one fabricates a perception of value and respect.

The madman's response reveals a deeply cynical and manipulative take on social interactions and power. To him, a person's importance isn't in any intrinsic worth but rather in their ability to build an appearance, a piece of "theatre" that garners respect and attention. This idea of "manners" implies an ability to put on a show, to control how others perceive you, making you appear as someone worthy of notice.

His mention of "linguistics and pronunciation" as vital elements underscores his belief that the surface details are crucial to building this illusion. The madman suggests that it's these manners alone that determine whether someone is deemed "valuable" or not, effectively rendering authenticity redundant or non-existent. In summing up his theory, the madman projects his own life philosophy: controlling perceptions and manipulating impressions are the true tools of power and domination—a view that justifies his own manipulative strategies and disdain for those who lack his skills.

The analyst, seeking clarity, presses on with a pointed question:

Analyst: —So you claim you could modify reality, by altering people's perceptions?

The madman fixes him with a stare, and with a slight shake of his head, he answers, weighing each word carefully:

Madman: —No, doctor, I can't change reality itself. Reality's built on a network of perceptions and structures people treat as fundamental. But I can certainly shift someone's perception in a given moment. Though, of course, the results depend on how each person interprets what they see.

He pauses, smiling with a hint of complicity, then adds, in a tone verging on the sardonic:

Madman: —Some things are simple enough, like figuring which breed of dog is bigger, a schnauzer or a greyhound. Trying to convince someone the greyhound's smaller would be pointless, even daft. But there are other cases, doctor, where one might insist on something a bit more ambiguous, like saying the schnauzer's got a better nose than the greyhound. Some poor fool might believe it, or at least someone who's heard the greyhound couldn't sniff out a prime steak.

The analyst listens, trying to anticipate where this comparison is leading. The madman continues, his tone now colder, more calculated:

Madman: —Mr Kendall was like a scrappy, clumsy greyhound. My job, after meeting him and Ms McBride —the one with the ankle tattoos— was to make Kendall look like a proper greyhound, someone the old-moneyed types would want to back. —He pauses, then adds with a nearly ironic smile—. And that, doctor, is hardly illegal... if that was your concern.

The analyst watches the madman, noting how his comparison turns Kendall into a malleable object, a "greyhound" that can be reshaped to fit the expectations and perceptions of those around him. In the madman's mind, he's not changing reality but rather adjusting a person's appearance so they slide neatly into a narrative others will accept without a second thought, all while he manoeuvres perceptions to his own advantage.

The madman's response underscores his knack for manipulating perception without the need to alter reality itself. To him, reality is immutable, but the perception of it is highly pliable, especially in matters that are ambiguous or open to personal interpretation. By explaining his comparison between the schnauzer and the greyhound, the madman crafts a metaphor about manipulation: some things are undeniable and cannot be changed, but in other cases, perception can easily be skewed.

He likens Kendall to a "scrawny greyhound," highlighting his apparent lack of worth and status. His mission, as he explains, was to make Kendall appear respectable and trustworthy in social circles—a "betting greyhound" others might admire and support. In his eyes, this isn't a lie or a distortion of the truth; rather, it's a recalibration of perception that breaks no law, even if it exists in a moral grey area. His response reveals that the madman doesn't view his manipulative actions as ethically questionable but as a game where reality remains intact while he plays with others' expectations, a form of control he considers his right and unique skill.

The madman, now immersed in his memories, explains his point with an almost obsessive precision, every word accompanied by gestures that emphasize his meticulous attention to detail.

Madman: "You see, doctor, when I was a boy, my mother always ensured the hems of my trousers stopped at just the right place so the shoelaces barely peeked out. The socks must never, ever be seen. The trouser crease needed to be razor-sharp—one single, clean line, no flaws."

As he speaks, he gestures to his own attire, proudly illustrating each detail with scrupulous exactitude.

Madman: "Take the jacket length, for instance. It should align with a closed fist's length. No hideous 'mother wrinkle' at the back, and the armholes must fit just so—too big, and the jacket looks small, giving a grotesque effect. I've always preferred Italian cotton shirts and silk ties."

He pauses, as if mulling over something obvious yet incomprehensible to most, then continues with a hint of superiority.

Madman: "Of course, most people wouldn't know whether a shirt's Italian or a tie's silk. For them, such details are trivial. But people like me, who've learned to judge and appreciate these things all our lives, know when we're seeing something genuine. Yet everyone, doctor, can tell if a shirt's immaculate and crisply ironed."

The madman savours his own precision, steering the conversation towards a final point:

Madman: "And shoes, doctor, shoes must always be clean and gleaming. The shinier, the more elegant. Have you seen the expressions of people when they notice someone with dirty shoes? There's only one reaction—disgust."

The analyst listens, noting how the madman uses these seemingly trivial details to construct a perception of superiority and respect. To him, every aspect of attire isn't merely a matter of style but a symbol of discipline and value—a criterion by which to judge others and reaffirm his own sense of control and superiority.

The madman's fixation on appearance reveals a worldview in which external details serve as indicators of character and status. His obsession with neatness and precision reflects a philosophy where every detail counts in building a solid, respectable image. To him, style is a means to manipulate how others perceive him, a tool to earn their respect or disdain.

The reference to "disgust" for those who neglect their shoes shows how he uses these standards of appearance as absolute measures of worth. In his mind, people aren't judged by who they are but by how they present themselves. Thus, the standards of dress his mother instilled have, for him, become a symbol of power and control: he who masters his appearance also controls how others perceive him.

This personal code of style and discipline reinforces his conviction of superiority, allowing him to scorn those who don't meet his standards as inferior or, indeed, unworthy of respect.

The analyst, trying to grasp the madman's logic, asks a provocative question:

Analyst: "So, according to you, with a well-polished pair of shoes, Mr Kendall could have walked into the House of Commons and demanded a hundred million pounds?"

The madman takes a moment to respond. With a ritualistic calm, he pulls a mint from his pocket, unwraps it without touching it with his fingers, and pops it into his mouth, biting down until a faint crunch is audible. Then he finally replies:

Madman: "In theory, yes. Though, of course, polished shoes are only the beginning. He'd also need a crisp white shirt, a decent watch, and a fountain pen—new but not entirely unused. Those are the first steps; then there's the right speech and a proper haircut." He smirks wryly. "We can't very well turn a common mechanic into some Lord of Lexington on hard times."

He pauses, as if the mention of a "mechanic" reminds him of something unpleasant.

Madman: "My ex-wife's father, who—as I mentioned—was ugly and later got fat, was also a mechanic. People could tell, you know? He never could trim his nails properly or keep them clean. Quite inexplicable, considering that by the time I met him, he was a... gigolo."

The analyst regards him, his expression reflecting a mixture of puzzlement and disapproval. Then he interjects with a hint of reproach:

Analyst: "Are you saying you despised your father-in-law simply because he was a mechanic?"

The madman sighs, his expression unflappable, and answers calmly, as if explaining something elementary.

Madman: "I didn't find him despicable for being a mechanic, doctor. I found him despicable for being a gigolo, living off an old woman who carted him around the world... nearly thirty years his senior."

His words hang in the air, loaded with a disdain that transcends mere appearance or occupation. The analyst watches him, sensing that, to the madman, dignity and respect aren't merely tied to appearance but rather to a "code" that values independence, dominance, and, in his own warped view, a form of "honour" that scorns any form of dependence or apparent lack of control.

The madman's response reveals a rigid and complex morality, where dignity is measured not only by outward appearance but by a conception of independence and control. For him, the contempt towards his father-in-law doesn't come from the fact that he was a mechanic, but from the way he lived like a "pimp," meaning he relied on an older woman for his livelihood and status. This, in his view, represents a lack of autonomy and a deviation from his own ideal of superiority and self-control.

In his logic, any sign of dependence or subordination is a reason for disdain. The comparison between Kendall and a "Lord of Lexington" highlights this perspective: it's not just about appearing elegant, but about adhering to a code of conduct that, in his mind, defines who deserves respect and who doesn't. The "facade" and "manners" he refers to are, for him, merely an aspect of something deeper, an outward sign of internal discipline that despises any form of weakness or dependence.

This moral code he imposes reveals that, in the madman's mind, life is a stage where each person must play a role of independence and control, where any sign of weakness or dependence becomes an unforgivable flaw.

The madman suddenly pauses in his story, seemingly reevaluating his words. He changes the tone of his speech, with a hint of mild reflection and mockery.

Madman: —Maybe, deep down, it wasn't so bad that my ex father-in-law was a pimp. In fact, it would've been a good life if he'd known how to be the pimp of an attractive woman, one of those between 30 and 50 years old. The real problem was the decrepitude of the woman who kept him... and his ineptitude, of course, as he was just a fourth-rate pimp.

The analyst, overwhelmed by the harshness and disdain in the madman's words, almost blurts out a question without thinking, seeking to understand a bit more about his worldview.

Analyst: —And why did you end your relationship with your "fat and ugly ex-wife"?

The madman immediately interrupts him, a look of disgust crossing his face, as if he'd detected an offense in the phrasing of the question.

Madman: —Doctor, I told you clearly, she was "ugly and then fat." Don't twist the semantics; phrasing it like that implies her ugliness was due to her fatness, and that wasn't the case. When she was with me, she was always ugly, and that was tolerable. I chose her knowing she was ugly: a Caucasian with small eyes, a thin nose, a prominent septum... the only decent thing was her mouth, but with such a short chin that it lacked grace. —He pauses, as if recalling a bitter detail—. But then, after we separated, she became fat, and that was the end of it.

The analyst listens attentively, as the madman settles back on the couch, and with a tone of pride, continues.

Madman: —Why did our relationship end? I suppose I got bored of her. So, I modulated her reality... I made her mother believe that her "freedom" and "realisation" as an independent woman were exactly what she deserved. Deep down, her mother did the dirty work; I just played the suffering one. Morally, I also had the advantage of presenting myself as the abandoned one.

The madman smiles with a cold satisfaction, as if this confession of manipulation were just another anecdote, a display of his ability to rewrite the narrative to his benefit. For him, the breakup wasn't an act of unlove, but a piece of manipulation carried out with precision, where the emotions of others were simply pawns in a power game he controlled at his convenience.

In this explanation, the madman shows his skill at manipulating the perceptions of those around him, projecting a version of events where he always holds the moral advantage. For him, the relationship and its end weren't acts of love or unlove, but a series of calculated maneuvers in which his ex-wife, her mother, and himself were actors in a script he'd written. His ability to "modulate reality" doesn't just imply control of actions, but a careful manipulation of others' perceptions, shaping their emotions and intentions for his own benefit.

The madman's indignation when correcting the analyst on the semantics reveals his obsession with narrative control: he won't allow the slightest deviation in how he presents his judgments, reflecting his sense of superiority and the importance he places on every detail of his story. In his view, the "abandonment" of the relationship becomes a personal achievement, where he gains the moral high ground and emotional independence, while his ex-wife and her family are left trapped in a reality he personally constructed.

The analyst, still baffled by the madman's confessions, throws a direct question, trying to provoke him.

Analyst: —So, do you recognise yourself as a manipulator of people?

The madman responds without hesitation, dismissing the label with an almost casual tone.

Madman: —No, none of that. If you want some frankness, doctor, I'd say I'm just a simple madman... a madman with luck.

The analyst, intrigued by the apparent contradiction, presses a little further.

Analyst: —Really? Don't tell me a person like you believes in luck.

The madman flashes a faint smile and responds with a tone of slight reverence, as if speaking about something sacred.

Madman: —Fortune is a goddess, doctor. As a deity, I think it's worth giving her her due place. —He pauses, gauging the analyst's reaction, and continues—. Don't you consider yourself fortunate? Every day we face natural causes that could end us, since we were children... and here we are, aren't we? We've survived.

The analyst listens, realising that the madman attributes his success and survival not to his actions or abilities, but to a kind of favourable destiny, an intervention he interprets as "fortune." For the madman, luck isn't mere chance, but a higher entity he respects and recognises as responsible for the favourable circumstances surrounding him.

The madman shuns the idea of being a "manipulator" of people, preferring to see himself as someone whose life has been guided by "fortune." For him, luck is not a random force, but something almost divine, a "goddess" that grants certain favours and whom he deems worthy of respect. This concept allows him to justify his success and actions without bearing the burden of manipulation, as if his influence over others were simply a consequence of good fortune rather than a calculated intention.

The madman projects the image of someone who has survived and prospered thanks to the intervention of this "goddess of fortune." This perspective allows him to reject the idea that he manipulates others, as in his mind, his position and achievements are the result of an external force. In this way, he distances himself from any direct responsibility, shifting the weight of his successes and actions onto the influence of a higher power, a concept that enables him to move through the world with a confidence he justifies through his own "luck."

The analyst, determined to get clear answers, insists on his question, seeking some form of acceptance from the madman.

Analyst: —I was asking about manipulation... do you consider yourself fortunate when it comes to manipulating people?

The madman calmly settles back in his chair. He stretches his arms and adjusts the shirt and sleeves of his jacket, as if preparing a carefully calculated response.

Madman: —No, doctor, I don't think my fortune is any greater than anyone else's. —He pauses for a prolonged moment, carefully measuring his words—. In fact... I think I have a technique. I've developed a methodology of actions learned and perfected through planning and repetition, until achieving a kind of mastery. That's the process, don't you think?

The analyst picks up on the precision in the madman's words, aware that he's avoiding the word "manipulation" and prefers to describe his behaviour as a skill honed through practice. The analyst then poses another question:

Analyst: —Did you use that "perfection and mastery" with... Mr. Kendall?

The madman answers immediately, without hesitation, as if the answer were obvious:

Madman: —Yes. I use it in everything I do, or at least in the vast majority of things. Observation is always the first step.

He stares at the analyst, his eyes fixed and calculating, continuing in a slow, almost didactic tone:

Madman: —Observing people allows you to understand their weaknesses, their little habits, their hidden desires. It's in those details that a structure of control is built. Repetition and perfection are the art of influencing without the other person realising.

The analyst watches in silence, sensing that the madman has turned the concept of manipulation into something he considers almost an art. For the madman, it's not about luck, but a rigorously cultivated skill, a refined technique that enables him to guide others' decisions and perceptions with calculated precision.

The madman avoids the word "manipulation," instead using terms like "technique" and "methodology" to describe his actions. This choice of words suggests he views his deeds as something objective and professional, a skill he's perfected through practice. By attributing his abilities to "mastery" rather than "fortune," the madman redefines manipulation as a subtle and disciplined art, more a science than a malicious intention.

The statement that "observation is the first step" reveals that the madman considers analysing people an essential tool for exercising control. For him, the success of this "methodology" lies in detecting others' vulnerabilities and patterns, using this knowledge to influence imperceptibly. In his view, manipulation isn't a random or chance act; it's a precise process where perfection and repetition are the means to achieve near-total dominance over others' perceptions and will.

The analyst, determined to get a concrete answer, asks another question:

Analyst: —So, did you manage to "get the hundred million pounds from Parliament" using your refined technique, as you've done in similar situations before?

The madman calmly shakes his head and responds firmly, taking his time to clarify his role.

Madman: —No, actually, I didn't get the hundred million pounds. That credit goes entirely to Mr. Kendall. —He pauses, almost as though recalling each step of a meticulously orchestrated process—. Mr. Kendall followed my instructions to the letter for nine weeks. Though the exact duration in months doesn't matter, I assure you, he was very disciplined.

The madman leans back in his seat and continues his account, detailing the "improvements" that helped transform Kendall's image.

Madman: —During those weeks, Mr. Kendall made an investment of £1,837 and some pennies. He didn't include this sum in the account book he carried everywhere, so I'm unaware of the source of that money. However, I know he used it to buy a grey wool suit and another three-piece suit, black, with a gunpowder grain. He also bought a second-hand French fountain pen and a second-hand Swiss watch, though I must admit it was in excellent condition. And, of course, two white cotton shirts. They weren't Italian or handmade, but I'll admit they were of sufficient quality to pass for those of a noble fallen on hard times.

He pauses, seemingly relishing the details, and continues:

Madman: —As for me, I gifted him a lovely Italian silk tie in a coffee colour, an old gift from a woman I met in Sussex, and an umbrella of exceptional quality. I also provided him with a box of superior Cuban cigars and 25 business cards printed on fine paper.

The analyst watches him, noting how the madman describes each item with obsessive precision, as if each detail were part of a well-thought-out strategy to project the image of success that Kendall needed. Finally, the madman adds:

Madman: —As for the shoes, someone —I suspect, with little doubt, it was Miss McBride— gifted him a pair of black shoes, locally made. They appeared second-hand and probably belonged to another man. Judging by the wear on certain details, I'd say those shoes had been kept for between thirteen and fifteen years.

The madman smiles slightly, satisfied with his explanation, while the analyst realises that the "transformation" of Kendall was a meticulously planned act of manipulation. For the madman, every accessory, every garment, and every gesture in Kendall's image were pieces of a calculated game to mould his perception in the eyes of others and give him a credibility he otherwise wouldn't have had.

The madman's description of Kendall's clothing and accessories reveals a careful and premeditated manipulation strategy. For the madman, Kendall's external appearance had to align with the standards of respect and success he hoped to gain from others. His account shows that, from his perspective, luxury items and aesthetic details are symbols that create the perception of value and power.

Each item —the wool suit, the Swiss watch, the French pen, even the business cards— becomes a calculated symbol meant to communicate a narrative of success and confidence. The gift of the silk tie and umbrella are, in this sense, personal contributions the madman considers essential to completing Kendall's transformation, giving him an image that would project authority and elegance.

The manipulation of perception in this context isn't seen by the madman as deception, but as a technique in which a person's value and credibility can be fabricated through carefully chosen details. This perspective reveals his belief that social reality is, to a large extent, a construct that can be shaped to create an ideal version of the person who inhabits it.

The analyst, trying to pinpoint the purpose behind Kendall's transformation, asks a question:

Analyst: —So, did you dress Mr. Kendall like a dandy?

The madman interrupts with a slight expression of disdain, adjusting his jacket sleeves and calmly shaking his head:

Madman: —I'm afraid you're mistaken, doctor. I simply stayed consistent with the story Mr. Kendall, Miss McBride, and I agreed upon in that old bar I mentioned earlier. —He pauses, remembering—. When I met Mr. Kendall, I noticed he didn't have the bearing needed to pass for one of those businessmen returned from India, America, or Tanzania. Those gentlemen, doctor, adopt a different accent to ours, an accent that marks them out and saves them from being mistaken for... people like you and me. To them, it would be offensive to sound like a fool from Notting Hill.

The madman smiles, pleased with his response, and continues describing his view of appearance and bearing:

Madman: —A mechanic's accent, on the other hand, sounds more like someone from Lexington. Their bearing is that of someone who's suffered the worst indignities of human life, working with metal, grease, iron, and steel tools. Tar soaks into their skin and no bleach can get rid of it. Moreover, these men tend to skip lotions, deodorants, scarves, and coats.

He pauses and then continues, almost admiringly:

Madman: —But the story of a fallen nobleman was perfect. A man who, though now an accountant or bank manager, has known what it is to work for survival. That weight makes him less dandyish, more real. That's how you build a convincing story.

THE ANALYST PICKS UP on the madman's disdain for those he deems "trained" for work and decides to steer the conversation in that direction.

Analyst: "So, you're saying that a man loses his freedom when he's forced to work?"

The madman smiles, pleased that the analyst is finally getting on the same page as his perspective, and replies with conviction:

Madman: "Not just saying it, Doctor. I'm backing it up with evidence. When have you ever seen an animal in its natural state working? Only circus-trained animals do tricks to earn their food. That proves that mechanics, like Mr. Kendall, are nothing more than trained monkeys, working without recognition."

He pauses for a moment, studying the analyst as if imparting a life lesson, then continues:

Madman: "Free men, like you and me, on the other hand, have the privilege of doing things that might seem pointless to a mechanic. For instance, we breakfast at the Geographical Society while mockingly ridiculing flat-earthers. Then we play a round of golf. And between us, Doctor... it's not that I'm a great player, but I wear these beautiful gold cufflinks with a golfer etched on them." —he rolls up his sleeves to show them— "And when luck's on my side and I'm invited to play, I always tell the story of when I beat the King in nearly perfect game."

The analyst listens closely, while the madman smiles, clearly enjoying his own story.

Madman: "Of course, no one asks which King, and there are plenty of them around Europe, right? So, everyone ends up satisfied, impressed that they've played golf with someone who beat a King. And if I don't have a good day on the course, I just shrug and say it was bad luck. But the myth remains, and most leave happy thinking they've played golf with a man who beat a King."

The madman leans back in his chair, content with his tale. For him, the truth doesn't matter; the story he projects is the real reality. In his view, freedom is the privilege of creating convincing narratives, shaping the perceptions of those around him.

The madman sees freedom as an existence free from the impositions of "servile" work, where the real privilege lies in engaging in activities that seem useless, merely to enjoy the perception they project onto others. His portrayal of Kendall is not just a strategy to access social and financial circles; for the madman, it is a social art form, a process of manipulation where every detail (the accent, the clothing, the stories) is calculated to create an attractive and convincing narrative.

The anecdote about the "King" illustrates this idea. It doesn't matter if the madman really beat a King at golf; what matters is the image he projects and the respect that fiction grants him. For the madman, the ability to make others believe his story is, in itself, a form of power and freedom.

In this view, reality isn't what happens, but what is told and perceived. The madman doesn't see his lack of concrete achievements as a hurdle; instead, he interprets his life as a series of narratives that others accept as truth, reaffirming his control over perception and the sense of freedom that, for him, defines the "superior men" as opposed to those who live under the servitude of work.

Continuing his tale, the madman describes the process of "educating" Mr. Kendall as a meticulous and necessary task to turn him into more than just a simple mechanic.

Madman: "Mr. Kendall had to learn to stop being a trained monkey. He needed to know the basics of golf, or at least be able to fake it. He had to pretend to know about horses, even if it was just a little. And above all, he had to pretend to be intelligent, even if he was just a nobody who knew nothing but metal and pressure pulleys. That's something free men, like us, couldn't care less about; that's what mechanics are for."

He pauses, adopting an almost didactic tone as he continues:

Madman: "Look, Doctor, members of the monarchy, even when they fall from grace, still maintain good habits. They know how to behave at the table, they can talk about philosophy, music, painting, sculpture, and, naturally, women. A man, Doctor, always needs to know about women."

The madman smiles, pleased with himself, and continues with a tone that blends cynicism with conviction:

Madman: "Luckily, even though he was a mechanic, Mr. Kendall knew the basics about women. He knew that diamonds are given to win a woman over and 'churumbelas' whenever they have a child." —The madman leans towards the analyst as though sharing a secret— "You must love them just enough, Doctor, and get them talking as much as possible. That way, you'll always have control."

The analyst watches, sensing a darker, more utilitarian view of relationships in the madman's words. The madman, however, seems to enjoy the effect his words have and continues:

Madman: "But there was a problem, Doctor. Mr. Kendall didn't have a woman by his side. And everyone knows that a man without a woman is just a trained monkey or a mechanic. Even among those two... 'semantic fields,' as you would say, it's frowned upon not to have a woman. People always speculate about the sexuality of a man who has no partner."

The analyst, sensing an opportunity, interrupts with curiosity:

Analyst: "Are you suggesting that Mr. Kendall had a different preference?"

The madman, almost indignantly, responds immediately:

Madman: "No, God no, Doctor. Mr. Kendall had a clear interest in Miss Stephany McBride. But she, being as stupid as she was, thought Kendall's interest was only in the money he planned to get from Parliament."

The madman observes the analyst, satisfied with his answer, as if he believes he has cleared up any confusion. For him, transforming Kendall into a "free" man required not just the right appearance and some social knowledge, but also the power to project a complete life, including the perception of having a woman by his side, something that, according to him, would complete the image of someone worthy of trust and influence.

The madman describes the process of "educating" Kendall not as mere teaching but as molding, where every detail — from basic golf skills to interactions with women — becomes a tool to create a perception of value and status. His insistence that "a man always needs to know about women" and that female companionship is essential to avoid suspicion reveals a rigid, socially-driven view of masculinity that the madman believes to be unchangeable.

THE IDEA OF "LOVING little" and "making them talk as much as possible" reveals a controlling mindset where relationships, for the madman, are not based on affection or mutual respect but on a dynamic of power and subordination. This logic of dominance also defines his insistence that Kendall needed a woman to complete his image, projecting a narrative that would lift him from the despised role of the "trained monkey" or "mechanic" and transform him into someone "free," on par with those who, as he believes, can move in circles of power and influence.

The madman, immersed in his story, details how he set about creating an aura of mystery and prestige around Mr. Kendall, using every connection and resource at his disposal.

Madman: —Actually, Mr. Kendall didn't think he could get the money from Parliament. The only one who was sure of that was me. Kendall, for his part, played along with Miss McBride because he had an interest in her, and that project kept them united in a rather precarious partnership. —He pauses, enjoying the effect of his words, and continues—. When I started advising him, Mr. Kendall began dressing properly and, thanks to my influence, started frequenting places like the chess club and the Geographical Society.

The analyst takes an interest in the detail:

Analyst: —So, Kendall played chess?

The madman looks at him almost pityingly and shakes his head:

Madman: —No, not at all. Only free men play cards and chess; that's logical. How could he play chess if he never had an interest in anything other than gears and grease? However, I must say Mr. Kendall had excellent taste in scotch and an incredible ability to drink it, something that, in our case, was a technical advantage.

The madman pauses, adjusting his posture, and continues his story:

Madman: —I had an old friendship with Sir William Stingler, as you're probably aware, the island's chess champion. Before Kendall started visiting the room where Stingler used to play, I took the opportunity to have lunch with him and mention that I'd be absent for a few weeks. I explained that I didn't want to make a fool of myself in front of a foreign champion.

The madman smiles, pleased with the memory, and continues:

Madman: —When a man is really good at something, doctor, he becomes curious as soon as he hears that there's someone just as good or better in his field, whether it's with women, sports, or finances. Chess players, of course, are no exception. On one occasion, I almost beat Stingler myself: a subtle move with the queen and it would've been checkmate. However, I realised that if I won, I'd be forced to keep playing and eventually he'd realise my victory was nothing but beginner's luck.

Analyst: —And what did you do?

Madman: —I pretended, doctor, subtly. I made a sign to Stingler with my eyes, revealing my next move. He understood; there was a slight blink as he wiped the sweat from his forehead. In the end, he won the game, and everything was fine, maintaining the stability that men of tradition so value. But privately, over breakfast the next day, I reminded him, humbly, that I could have beaten him, and that it was his cunning that saved him from defeat. At first, he resisted admitting it, but then he thanked me briefly. That's how, doctor, I ensured a lasting victory, without the need for fleeting glory lasting only a few minutes.

The madman smiles and continues, describing how he used this anecdote to weave an intriguing story around Kendall:

Madman: —I told Stingler I'd met a fellow named Kendall, who had swept the board in less than a minute, and that no one in France had beaten him. That piqued his curiosity, of course, because a man like Stingler can't resist competition. I mentioned that Kendall hardly ever played with others, and that only increased his interest. But the best part was when I told him a story about Kendall and a Frenchman named Heyraud. According to my tale, during a game in Lyon, Kendall had pushed Heyraud to the limit, and when he finally won, Heyraud got up, took three steps, and collapsed, struck by a heart attack.

The analyst looks at him, astonished, while the madman smiles, pleased with the reaction.

Madman: —It's funny, doctor, but men who enjoy humiliating others often have a natural inclination for gossip. Stingler was no exception; the story fascinated him. I held his gaze while assuring him I'd read all about it in a sensationalist newspaper from Lyon. The legend was set, and all I had to do was plant it in the mind of a man eager to believe it.

The madman leans back, crossing his legs and enjoying his cigarette, pleased with the story he has woven and the analyst's incredulous expression.

The madman's narrative reveals a masterful ability to manipulate perception and build stories that project power and mystery. In his view, reputation is not built solely on real skills but on carefully crafted myths that others accept and spread. The story of the fatal chess match in Lyon is a clear example: the madman transforms Kendall into a mythical figure, someone worthy of respect and fear, in order to gain influence in circles that would otherwise reject him for his humble origins.

The manipulation of Stingler through the "secret" of his lost game and the story of Kendall reflects a strategy in which the madman uses others' desires and egos as tools. Stingler, eager to protect his reputation and fascinated by the idea of an equal or better rival, falls into the trap. The madman doesn't just manipulate facts; he manipulates emotions, pride, and curiosity, thus constructing an alternative reality that allows him to transform Kendall into a "free man" of respectable appearance.

This ability to weave stories and project power through illusion is, for the madman, the true key to freedom and control. It's not about whether Kendall is a great chess player; what matters is that, in the eyes of others, Kendall appears to be extraordinary. This distinction between the real and the perceived is at the core of the madman's philosophy, who sees the manipulation of perception as the ultimate tool for shaping and dominating his environment.

The analyst, disheartened by the harshness of the story, looks at the madman with a hint of disappointment:

Analyst: —So, you lied to "your friend" Stingler...

The madman lets out a slight laugh and responds calmly:

Madman: —I never said he was "my friend." If he'd been my friend, doctor, I would've beaten him at chess. You grant friends that kind of satisfaction, and sometimes, lessons.

Analyst: —Why? —asks the analyst, intrigued.

Madman: —Because I couldn't have blackmailed a friend like I did Stingler. Sir William, on the other hand, I made him invite me to lunch over and over again, up to a thousand times, including this one where we discussed about Mr. Kendall. Stingler feared I could actually beat him at his one talent, so every time I hinted at sitting down to play with him, he invited me to lunch, and I, of course, accepted. I usually had crab and orange juice; it was a fair price. But that day, I decided to settle for a boiled egg, a slice of bread, and a coffee.

Analyst: —And does that have any significance? —asks the analyst, growing increasingly despondent.

The madman, adopting a tone of absolute seriousness, nods.

Madman: —Of course it does. Had I ordered crab and orange juice, which cost nearly £30 more, Stingler would have known I was just bluffing. But by sticking to such a simple breakfast, I made it clear that my concern wasn't the food, but the content of our message. It gave depth and credibility to the story about Kendall being a great chess player.

The analyst listens in silence, while the madman continues explaining his strategy with satisfaction.

Madman: —My "absence" from the club wasn't because I refused to face Kendall, but because I needed him to use my membership. It was a fair investment. And at the end of our breakfast, Stingler admitted that killing someone over a chess game was a good reason to stop playing, though not necessarily to stop watching others do it. It's like those football fans, doctor, who've ended up with a destroyed knee but still torture themselves with the nostalgia of watching others play.

The madman leans back, content, while the analyst realises that every decision the madman made, right down to the detail of a simple breakfast, was a piece in a meticulously orchestrated game of manipulation. For the madman, every aspect, every choice—even something as trivial as breakfast—was a tool to sustain his narrative and create an air of mystery and respect around Kendall.

The madman's account of his strategy with Sir William Stingler reveals his knack for crafting a story from seemingly insignificant details. Instead of relying on objective facts, the madman uses trivial elements—like the type of breakfast—to convey subtleties that add depth and authenticity to his tale. For him, these details are what lend credibility to the manipulation, allowing his version of events to resonate with believability.

The choice of a simple breakfast over an expensive crab dish reinforces his intent: by projecting an image of austerity, the madman makes his story about Kendall seem more authentic. In his mind, the economy of his choices gives Stingler the impression that his words carry serious weight, thus creating the illusion that Kendall was a mysterious and formidable figure.

This detailed strategy of manipulation, where even the breakfast menu serves a specific purpose, demonstrates the madman's mastery in controlling others' perceptions. To him, manipulation isn't just about lying; it's about carefully weaving every element of the context to create an all-encompassing illusion that others accept as truth.

The madman, after a pause and a sip from his flask, resumes his tale with the intensity of someone unveiling a crucial piece in a complex game.

Madman: —As I was saying, the first day Mr. Kendall walked into the chess room, I was nervous. I made it very clear in my instructions: he was to order a scotch with two ice cubes, no more, no less. Drink it within a precise time, between three and eight minutes; neither too fast nor too slow. Then, he had to wander between the tables, squinting as if analysing every move on the board, as if comparing the pieces to the bands of a complex engine.

The analyst listens, hanging on every detail, while the madman continues:

Madman: —My plan was for Stingler to approach him, call him by his last name, as if they were old acquaintances, and invite him to lunch. Kendall was to order crab and orange juice, no "thank you" or "sir"; just treat him as an equal. This would catch the attention of Sir Arthur Standish, a tall man, slender as a pole, with an excellent eye. Standish would boast to Kendall about his position as secretary to a member of the House of Commons, and Kendall was to reply that, with a hundred million pounds, he could restore the honour of his family and of all of Britain.

Analyst: —Obviously, it wasn't as straightforward as it seems.

Madman: —No, doctor, it wasn't easy at all —the madman admits, taking a sip from his dark leather-bound steel flask—. Sometimes, when I talk a lot, my throat gets dry.

Analyst: —Would you like some coffee?

Madman: —No, doctor, I'd rather be poisoned before drinking coffee —he replies with a bitter smile—. Coffee makes me nervous, and tea messes with my blood pressure. I prefer this. —He drinks from his flask and then wipes his mouth with a blue and gold handkerchief that matches his tie.

After another sip, the madman resumes his explanation:

Madman: —Kendall made six visits to the chess room before Standish finally took the bait. And while he followed my instructions, there was no guarantee the effect would be immediate. Sometimes I doubt Kendall did each gesture to perfection, but in the end, Standish fell for it. And that's when a new and complex scenario began.

The analyst offers a chocolate, which the madman accepts without hesitation.

Madman: —Do you know why this all worked, doctor?

Analyst: —No, I can't imagine —the analyst admits, genuinely intrigued.

Madman: —It was the contempt. Kendall, as a mechanic, had an innate disdain for those "educated" people who waste their time with board games and little pieces of ivory and onyx. The interesting thing was that, by following my advice to the letter, those very same men started interpreting his contempt as that of a noble fallen from grace, someone from a rural region, someone... let's say, from a lineage lost in time.

The analyst listens with growing curiosity as the madman continues, pleased with his narration:

Madman: —In the end, Kendall got something that seemed impossible: an invitation to the opera.

Analyst: —And there, he met Lavander Sthaldt?

Madman: —No. Miss Sthaldt is... a well-known businesswoman from the streets of London, in an area where, either you box or you're a "businesswoman." I doubt you frequent that part of the city, and I don't blame you, I haven't been there in years. But I know people who do. Lavander was the only one I could think of to help Kendall in his days of rage.

Analyst: —Days of rage? —the analyst asks, confused, lifting his tea cup—. What do you mean by that?

The madman smiles, and with a slow, almost reverent tone, responds:

Madman: —It's the title of a Latin poem, "Dies Irae"... it's not classical Latin, you know? Have you noticed its metre? It's trochaic. —The madman closes his eyes and softly recites—. Dies irae, dies illa...

The analyst watches the madman, realising that for him, "days of rage" weren't just a literary reference, but a symbol of the tension and darkness surrounding his plans. The madman speaks of these "days of rage" as if they were an integral part of his power play, a preparation for moments of chaos and confrontation that required not only strategy, but a cold and calculating calm.

In this part of the interview, the madman uses the reference of "Dies Irae" to symbolise the dark, calculated backdrop of his plan with Kendall. For him, "Day of Wrath" is a metaphor for those moments when control and chaos collide, when people are pushed to the brink of their emotions or wills. By alluding to "Dies Irae," the madman not only adds a tone of gravity to his tale, but frames his actions as part of an almost poetic structure, where manipulation and contempt are essential elements of a grand work.

The detail with the scotch, the breakfast, and the visits to the chess room reflects his conviction that every gesture is crucial to building a convincing story. For the madman, Kendall had to project the image of someone who despised those he considered beneath him, and it was this disdain that ultimately led his contemporaries to mistake him for a noble fallen from grace. This narrative reveals the madman's ingenuity in using perception and emotions—specifically contempt and fascination with mystery—as tools to sculpt the reality of those around him, leading them to accept as truth what is, in reality, a carefully constructed lie.

The madman, enjoying another chocolate offered by the analyst, continues his tale, detailing the preparations necessary for Mr. Kendall to attend the opera as someone of class and nobility.

Madman: —It must be clear, doctor, that receiving an invitation to the opera is one of the most serious events that can happen in a person's life, and there are certain rules that cannot be ignored. The first is the tuxedo: one must wear a bow tie and cummerbund. Any decent man knows how to tie a bow tie, but a mechanic, of course... —The madman pauses, rolling his eyes with contempt—. The next rule is that, if you're a man over 14, you must attend with a woman who isn't your mother.

The analyst nods, understanding that the madman was facing a considerable logistical and social challenge in transforming Kendall into someone acceptable in those circles.

Madman: —The tuxedo was sorted out easily with 31 quid and two shillings, which covered the rent and deposit. And as you can imagine, no one who aspires to look like royalty turns up in just any old car. It had to be a Rolls-Royce. Luckily, among my contacts, I found an old acquaintance, Andreson Zvensky, who owed me seven quid and a favour. I asked him for a white Rolls, and that's how Mr. Kendall and Lavander arrived at the opera.

The madman pulls out a small, yellowing, worn notebook from his portfolio, almost as if to emphasise his point, and flips through it quickly.

Madman: —This agenda is always with me, doctor. I keep every contact, every favour owed. Zvensky, for example, turned out to be the key to Kendall arriving with the right style.

Analyst: —And Miss Lavander? What did she think of the opera?

Madman: —Ah, doctor, don't think it was easy. Lavander is a woman who... well, she has no interest in that sort of thing. But I asked her to do her best to play her part, and she agreed. In the end, it's all about maintaining appearances and making sure others see exactly what we want them to see.

The madman leans back in his chair, visibly pleased with the precision of his preparation. To him, every detail—from the bow tie to the car model—was essential in constructing the façade around Kendall, projecting the image of a man of honour and position. Lavander's presence completed the picture, suggesting that Kendall was not just respectable, but someone accompanied by a highly attractive woman, someone who validated him in those exclusive circles.

The madman's account reflects his obsession with detail and his belief in the importance of projecting a perfect image to influence how others perceive you. To him, every external element—the tuxedo, the bow tie, the Rolls-Royce—was a symbol communicating social status and a narrative that society would accept without question. Choosing Lavander as his companion completed the picture, and her presence at the opera further validated Kendall as someone worthy of admiration.

This manipulation, in the madman's mind, was not just a lie, but an artistic construction. By including Lavander and ensuring that every detail was meticulously planned, the madman reinforced the idea that reality was simply a matter of perception. To him, appearances were all that truly mattered, as they determined how others judged a person and, ultimately, what opportunities and recognition they received. This philosophy, where the substance is irrelevant if the form is perfect, underscores his belief that life, at its core, is a game of appearances that he can control and shape to his advantage.

The analyst, intrigued by the influence the madman had over people like Lavander, asks a question:

Analyst: —How did you manage to convince Lavander to attend the opera? She doesn't seem like an easy woman to deal with.

The madman, almost amused, responds with calculated calm:

Madman: —Actually, doctor, I beg to differ. Lavander's a very simple girl. Like all women, she loves to show off, and from that angle, you can handle her however you like.

Analyst: —Was that how your wife was? The ugly one, then the fat one?

Madman: —No, not at all. My wife was shy and hated being scrutinised by others. Lavander, on the other hand, loves to flaunt herself. Her golden hair, her green eyes, her figure in a tight dress... although completely inappropriate for the occasion, it's something she enjoys.

The analyst watches the madman, who seems to delight in the image he's constructed of Lavander. Intrigued, he asks:

Analyst: —Didn't you find that dress uncomfortable?

The madman smiles with an expression bordering on malicious satisfaction:

Madman: —Not at all, doctor. I wanted others to desire her, to look at her with intensity, almost with longing. The best way to do that was by "showing a little bit." —He pauses, gauging the effect of his words—. By provoking desire in others, she became a symbol of power and attraction, which gave Mr. Kendall an image of prestige and... respectable desirability.

For the madman, Lavander's image was not just about appearance; it was a tool of manipulation in his plan. He knew that her provocative presence would capture everyone's attention and generate a sort of social validation around Kendall, turning him into someone seemingly admired and coveted.

The madman's response reveals his understanding of social psychology and his ability to manipulate desire as a tool of control. To him, Lavander's display was a calculated strategy that would make Kendall the centre of attention. With her seductive image, Lavander wouldn't just attract looks; she would also give Kendall an air of success and status, suggesting that he was a man who could attract a woman desired by everyone.

The madman's response shows that, for him, people aren't complex individuals with their own desires and limits; they're pieces on a chessboard that can be positioned to create a specific impression. The manipulation of desire here isn't just a whim, but a technique that exploits the power of image, using Lavander's appearance as a tool to influence and generate respect for Kendall. This strategy underscores the madman's belief that external perception and the desire it creates can shape a person's reality, granting them a kind of authority and social value that they don't actually possess.

The madman, with a look of satisfaction and pride, reflects on the results of the opera evening:

Madman: —The opera outing was an absolute success, doctor. But, as usual, it also led to problems later on. For the first time, Mr. Kendall experienced what it really means to be human in the fullest sense. Meanwhile, Lavander, at last, had caught the attention of those she wanted to impress.

The analyst, curious about the reactions of the others involved, asks:

Analyst: —And Miss McBride? Wasn't she upset with you for orchestrating this… "lie"?

The madman smiles, pleased, and responds without a hint of doubt:

Madman: —Not at all. Miss McBride began to convince herself that the goal of securing a hundred million pounds from Parliament was actually possible, numerically feasible. Meanwhile, Mr. Kendall began to grasp what it meant to be "a fallen member of the British nobility."

Analyst: —And how can you be so sure of that?

The madman smiles fully for the first time, a touch of genuine pride in his expression, and replies:

Madman: —Because I know what it's like to take a human being to the heavens, and I also know what it's like to throw them into hell. I've dedicated my whole life to that, doctor. Kendall was finally recognised, his opinion became relevant. That week, he received four phone calls and eleven telegrams. People were asking for his advice on art appreciation, horse racing, and other topics, which, frankly, I can't remember now. It's not that they were insignificant; I just didn't pick up the phone, as you'd expect.

Analyst: —So, did Mr. Kendall answer the phone himself? —the analyst interrupts.

Madman: —No, not at all. Tell me, doctor, do you know any truly important man who answers the phone himself? That task was left to

Miss McBride, who, by the way, has a rather attractive voice when she's on the phone.

The analyst smiles faintly, but then asks with a touch of irony:

Analyst: —And your ex-wife, the one who was ugly at first and then got fat... did she have an attractive voice on the phone too?

The madman feigns slight annoyance and responds with disdain:

Madman: —No... not in the slightest. She never had the ability to answer a call on my behalf. Though McBride may have been stubborn and a bit thick, at least she was useful. —He pauses, sizing up the analyst, before continuing with a conspiratorial grin—. Lavander, on the other hand, asked me privately if there'd be another exit from the opera with my "little client." I assured her that Kendall would go to the racing club, and that got her excited. I also told her he'd walk in there with a bouquet of three hundred red roses, and that way, all the high society women in London would know she was the most desired woman in town.

The analyst, adopting an ironic tone, asks about the fulfilment of the promise:

Analyst: —And did Lavander ever go to the racing club?

The madman looks at him, as if offended by the suggestion he wouldn't keep his word, and responds with complete conviction:

Madman: —Of course she did, doctor. I had given my word, and Lavander would go, no question. Besides, she arrived with a bouquet of 288 red roses, which was all I could find in London in the dead of winter. It wasn't cheap, and I had to call in a few favours.

He pauses, reliving the scene in his mind, and continues:

Madman: —That day, they arrived in the usual white Rolls, which half the city assumed belonged to Mr. Kendall. Lavander looked impeccable, in a white dress with lace sleeves and matching gloves, discreetly made up. She looked, doctor, like a bride walking into Westminster.

Analyst: —And what happened, essentially? —the analyst interrupts, showing a slight desperation.

The madman, unfazed, responds calmly:

Madman: —What had to happen. There wasn't a high-society lady in London who didn't look at Lavander with a mix of envy and disdain, and not a single gentleman present who didn't desire her, nor who didn't look at Mr. Kendall with admiration and, yes, with something that seemed like respect.

The madman smiles, clearly pleased, and adds:

Madman: —I was there too, though I had to settle for a dreadful jacket, as the one I usually wear to events like that was being worn by Kendall. I also had a French hat, which, after a good wash and dry cleaning, no one could guess I bought at a market in the suburbs, from my favourite seller, Tara Garnell, who's now a barista.

He pauses, a spark of excitement in his eyes, as if reliving the moment his plan came to life.

Madman: —That day, I knew my plan was about to come to fruition. Everything was going exactly as I had planned... though I must admit, doctor, I never thought Mr. Kendall would have the audacity to be so irreverent.

The analyst, picking up on the intrigue in the madman's words, raises an eyebrow, waiting for him to continue. For the madman, every detail of Lavander's grand entrance at the racing club was part of a carefully orchestrated performance, a construction of the image Kendall needed to cement his status. But Kendall's unexpected irreverence suggests that the plan may have led to consequences outside the madman's control, adding a new layer of tension to the unfolding events.

The madman's account of Lavander's arrival at the riding club reflects his obsession with the power of image and the manipulation of social perception. To him, every detail, from the dress and the bouquet of roses to the choice of car, was calculated to provoke envy, desire, and respect. In his mind, these carefully selected superficial gestures allow the shaping of Kendall and Lavander's social reality, presenting them as figures of status and class.

However, the mention of Kendall's "irreverence" suggests that the plan might have had unexpected effects. For the madman, absolute control is crucial, and Kendall's ability to act on his own introduces an element of risk. This potential "rebellion" from Kendall could be interpreted as a sign that the madman's manipulation has succeeded in turning him into someone who no longer feels confined by his original role, adding an unpredictable dimension to the outcome of the master plan.

The madman, absorbed in his tale, takes a sip of tea with milk while contemplating a biscuit on the porcelain plate before him. He pauses and bites into the biscuit, enjoying the moment's detail, then continues with his story:

Madman: —That day, Mr. Kendall and Lavander sat down for tea with Lord Munrouth and Miss Cover. —He pauses, then clarifies—. Lord Munrouth, doctor, was a close family friend of the Curzons. Yes, the Curzons, the ones who were Viceroys of India and, well, involved in certain scandals.

The madman smiles, relishing the memory of his preparation for the meeting.

Madman: —After a failed marriage of young Curzon to a wife... let's say, of an unconventional lineage, a hybrid of Kurdish and Amazonian, the scandal was about to erupt in high society. Of course, Lord Munrouth, being a moral leader in one of the Houses and the administrator of fortunes for the true royalty, knew that silence came at a high price.

The analyst listens, fascinated by the web of connections and the complexity of the environment the madman describes, as he continues:

Madman: —So, doctor, what could a mechanic and a "lady of the night" possibly talk about with a Lord who managed the finances of some of the most illustrious British families? I'd already solved that. First, they'd talk about machines. That's a subject Kendall mastered. He'd explain to Lord Munrouth that a nation's development depended on its specialisation in technology. He might openly criticise how few decent men in the country took an interest in pulleys or the tension between them. He could even instruct him on when to use coal and when to use electricity, all depending on industry.

The madman smiles, recalling the precision of his plan.

Madman: —Then, they'd move on to talk about war and its horrors. Kendall had been at the front, I'm not sure if with the Boers or in some other conflict; honestly, I never cared much about which war he'd been in. But Munrouth had also led troops in Africa in his youth. War, doctor, has a way of uniting men in a way peace never could. —He pauses and concludes—. So, after listening to this "patriot," Lord Munrouth would be fascinated. Kendall would become someone that, without a doubt, the Ministry of Industry and the businessmen's clubs should listen to.

The madman takes another sip of tea and continues:

Madman: —We practised the speech for three whole nights. I assured Mr. Kendall that I'd be close by, and if he dropped his tea cup, I'd be there to rescue him. Lavander, for her part, had to maintain a slight look of disdain at all times, smile courteously when necessary, and blink with a certain... voluptuousness if asked a question. Any response from her would be fine, it didn't matter if she said something silly; she just had to distract.

The analyst listens, captivated by the level of detail and precision in the preparation, but the madman adds a final remark tinged with a hint of regret:

Madman: —However, doctor, the one who wasn't considered in our equation was Miss Cover.

The analyst raises an eyebrow, sensing that Miss Cover introduced an unexpected factor into the madman's plan. The madman's ability to foresee each interaction and detail suggests meticulous manipulation, but Miss Cover's unforeseen intervention seems to have represented an obstacle he hadn't anticipated. This unforeseen presence promises to add tension to the story, making it clear that even the most perfect plans can be altered by the intervention of an uncontrollable element.

The madman's tale reveals his skill in manipulating situations through exhaustive planning. His strategy of preparing Kendall with topics such as technology and war, subjects that would resonate with Lord Munrouth, demonstrates his understanding of high society's interests and his ability to guide the perception of his interlocutors. The instructions given to Lavander to distract without truly engaging in the conversation add an element of subtlety and control, revealing his precision in manipulating social interactions.

Miss Cover's presence, however, represents an unexpected twist. In the madman's mind, everything is designed for Kendall and Lavander to move according to his instructions, projecting a calculated image of fallen nobility and intriguing allure. Miss Cover's intervention suggests a factor outside his control, posing a challenge to his absolute dominance over the stage he'd created. This unforeseen presence introduces vulnerability into the madman's plan, revealing that, although he believes he controls every detail, there is always the possibility of unpredictable elements interfering, testing his ability to adapt amidst the manipulation.

The madman, finishing the last biscuit from the porcelain plate decorated with green and gold, pauses before continuing, his tone now tinged with an almost reverent respect.

Madman: —Miss Cover… Do you know her?

Analyst: —No, not really. Well, I did see a picture of her in a high-society magazine once, though I'm not sure if we're talking about the same person —the analyst hesitates.

The madman grins maliciously and watches him intently.

Madman: —Well, well! We have here another secret admirer. —The madman smirks and continues—. Miss Cover, whose first name is Nicole, is like a pearl.

Analyst: —Is it because of her skin colour?

The madman raises his eyebrows and widens his eyes, surprised.

Madman: —No, not at all. I'm not racist... well, yes, but not in that way. —He pauses, as if carefully choosing his words—. Nicole is like a pearl because she's unique and has a perfect shape, with curves that accentuate that area where the back loses its name. She has a smile that captivates, and hazel eyes that snare anyone. But what really defines her, doctor, is that she's probably the most intelligent person on the entire Island.

The analyst watches the madman with growing interest, and the madman adds, as if revealing an important warning:

Madman: —And an intelligent woman is a dangerous woman. A woman like Nicole Cover can destroy any creation that "modulates reality."

The madman falls silent, allowing the tension of his words to settle. For him, Nicole Cover's intelligence represents a danger, not just for her ability to uncover the farce surrounding Kendall and Lavander, but because a woman like her possesses the power to see beyond appearances, to spot manipulations, and to dismantle any lie, no matter how sophisticated.

The madman sees in Nicole not just a threat to his plan, but a risk to his absolute control over the people he "modulates." His respect for her intelligence is accompanied by an implicit fear, for he knows that someone as perceptive as she is capable of detecting any deceit, any deviation from the reality he is so determined to build. To the madman, Nicole Cover's presence introduces a fundamental vulnerability: someone who could, if she chose, dismantle his carefully constructed world.

The respect and fear the madman expresses towards Nicole Cover reveal his recognition that, for the first time, he faces someone who could unravel his manipulations. For the madman, people are malleable pieces; however, a woman like Nicole, with a sharp mind and the ability to see beyond appearances, represents a dangerous anomaly. Comparing Nicole to a "pearl" is not merely aesthetic; her uniqueness lies in her intelligence, which makes her perception something unreachable for the madman, someone used to manipulating others with little resistance.

The phrase "an intelligent woman is a dangerous woman" encapsulates the madman's fear of losing control. Nicole is not just attractive or fascinating; she possesses a keen observation and analytical ability that makes her a threat to any "modulated reality" he creates. This presence introduces a dynamic of vulnerability in his power game, where, for the first time, he faces someone he cannot manipulate so easily, and who could, if she chose, expose his intricate farces.

The madman, with a touch of frustration in his voice, continues to recount the unexpected turn in his plan with Miss Cover.

Madman: —In situations like this, doctor, the only option is to use any excuse to deal with the obstacles. The original idea was that Miss McBride, with her natural clumsiness, would cause an "incident" that shouldn't pose much difficulty. She was supposed to approach Miss Cover with a glass of wine and accidentally spill it on the lapel of her suit. Yes, it might seem like a barbaric and cruel act, but it was justified.

The analyst watches him, understanding the coldness with which the madman planned to manipulate even the most trivial interactions.

Madman: —McBride would have to apologise profusely and offer to pay for the ruined clothes. Nicole would leave upset and somewhat disappointed, but our plan would remain safe. Even Mr. Kendall could take advantage of the situation by sending her a card of apology, excusing himself for his assistant's clumsiness.

The madman leans back, his tone revealing some exasperation.

Madman: —However, when I got up from my desk to give McBride precise instructions, I didn't consider that her natural clumsiness would be... too much. —He pauses and continues with a tone of resignation—. Instead of spilling the wine on Miss Cover, McBride actually tripped and tossed the glass into the air... for no reason at all. It was a spectacle, doctor, and the worst part was that I couldn't even bring my hands to my face to hide my expression; that would have been a dead giveaway. And, of course, you can't spill two glasses of wine at the same event; although it's not written anywhere, we all know that's inadmissible.

The madman shakes his head, still visibly upset by the failure of his strategy, and resumes the story.

Madman: —Nicole Cover, of course, stayed the whole afternoon, listening intently to the speech about war, mechanics, patriotism, and industry. But she didn't buy a single word, doctor. Not one.

The analyst observes the madman, seeing a mixture of frustration and respect on his face. Nicole had done what few could: she perceived the farce, remained unaffected by the spectacle, and resisted the manipulation the madman had so carefully orchestrated. For the madman, this failure marked a crack in his strategy; his inability to remove Nicole from the scene exposed the limited reach of his control in situations where his distraction tactic failed.

The failed attempt to manipulate Nicole Cover through McBride's clumsiness reveals both the madman's skill in planning every detail and the fragility of those plans when an unforeseen event intervenes. The madman had every move, every word of apology, and every consequence in mind, but McBride's clumsiness at the wrong moment broke the spell he was trying to cast. Instead of being a factor that contributed to distracting Nicole, the failed wine spill turned the situation into an event with no impact.

Nicole's reaction, where she listened to everything without being swayed, highlights her ability to see beyond appearances. For the madman, someone who can resist his manipulations and maintain a clear perception becomes a real threat, someone who could, if she chose, dismantle the castle of illusions he had built. Nicole's presence as a watchful, critical spectator introduces a vulnerability in his strategy, making it clear that there are people for whom the perception of truth is unshakable, and who are not dazzled by the superficial spectacle he so skilfully controls in most of his manipulations.

The madman, with a tone of slight bitterness, continues recounting the events that followed the evening at the country club.

Madman: —As if the situation couldn't get any worse, doctor, every time Mr. Kendall looked at Miss Cover, something in his eyes made me think he felt like he was in heaven, looking at an angel. An angel so beautiful that he couldn't concentrate on the plan. McBride noticed, and she was offended; she knew deep down she could get so much more from Kendall if he preferred her.

The madman shakes his head, as if contemplating the disaster of a machine failing at the most crucial moment, and continues.

Madman: —Later, in private, I confronted her and gave her a right earful about her stupidity. I explained that with her carelessness, she had jeopardised the whole operation and the stability of her relationship with Kendall. Kendall's interest in McBride had completely vanished.

Analyst: —So, even though that afternoon Lavander had won the admiration of London's high society...

Madman: —Exactly. Even though that woman, with her bunch of 288 red roses, had charmed half of London, she lost the one person who truly mattered. Because, doctor, I had done the impossible: I had convinced the members of the upper crust of this city that a mechanic born in the suburbs was one of the most cultured, intelligent, and knowledgeable people when it came to economics, finance, and industrial technology.

The madman pauses for a few seconds, letting the weight of his failed success sink in, then adds with a touch of resignation:

Madman: —However, Nicole Cover had a doubt, a reasonable doubt, if you will. And Miss McBride... she had one foot out the door.

The analyst observes, understanding the complexity of the situation: the madman had managed to convince the elite that Kendall was someone of great importance, but he hadn't foreseen the fragility of human feelings or the risks posed by Kendall's interest in Nicole Cover. What seemed like a total success had turned into a web of personal complications that threatened to unravel the operation. In his attempt to manipulate everyone's desires and perceptions, the madman discovered that there are factors —like love or genuine desire— that are beyond his control, and that even the most well-constructed lie can be vulnerable when confronted with the real emotions of the participants.

The madman's tale shows that despite his ability to shape perception and control every detail, some elements cannot be easily manipulated. The success of his plan —convincing the elite that Kendall was of great importance— was overshadowed by the unexpected intrusion of human feelings. Kendall's attraction to Nicole Cover, as well as McBride's jealousy, revealed that even the most meticulous plans can collapse when the participants develop genuine feelings that defy external manipulations.

The fact that Nicole Cover held doubts, coupled with McBride's threat of losing her position, suggests that the madman's strategy wasn't just vulnerable to mistakes, but to the unpredictability of real emotions. Though he can construct a convincing narrative for others, he can't prevent his "actors" from developing their own motivations, which introduces a fundamental fragility into any lie or farce dependent on the unpredictable nature of human feelings.

The madman, visibly irritated, continues venting about McBride's incompetence, while the analyst listens attentively, picking up on the disillusionment in his words.

Madman: —That very night, doctor, I lost it. Miss McBride's incompetence was beyond belief. I told her, did she need to rehearse just to spill a glass of water on someone? —He pauses, as though recalling the scene with bitterness—. I even threatened to call my ex-wife... yes, the one who was ugly and then got fat, to do that job. And believe me, doctor, for a moment I really thought my ex-wife would have been better than McBride at something as simple as that.

The analyst, intrigued, observes as the madman pauses, weighing his thoughts.

Madman: —I would have called my ex-wife if it weren't for the fact that she now teaches at a secondary school in a village about... 45 miles from here. A place with more cows than students. But then I remembered her ugliness and her weight, and well, doctor, that put me off asking her to teach McBride something as basic as tossing a glass of water.

The analyst smiles wryly, and without missing a beat, asks a question tinged with curiosity:

Analyst: —Did you and your wife argue much? The ugly and then fat one...

The madman looks at him, expressionless, as though the question has caught him slightly off guard.

Madman: —No, we never argued. —He pauses, eyeing the analyst with a calculated coldness—. One day, she just disappeared. Didn't give me any explanation. So, doctor, I feel morally justified in talking about her ugliness and her weight. She chose to leave without a word, so I choose to describe her as she was.

The analyst nods, realising that the madman uses this explanation as a justification for his disdain. For him, the disappearance of his ex-wife is the perfect excuse to strip her of any consideration and reduce her to the features he despises. In his view, there's no room for nuance or self-criticism; just a sense of betrayal that allows him to speak of her coldly.

The madman's narrative about his ex-wife reveals his tendency to dehumanise those he considers beneath him or who have failed to meet his expectations. For him, McBride's incompetence is unforgivable, and it leads him to question whether replacing her with his ex-wife, whom he also despises, would have been a better option. When describing her, he focuses on her physical flaws, as if these were a representation of her character or the "betrayal" he perceives in her leaving him.

The coldness with which the madman describes the relationship suggests a total lack of empathy. For him, relationships are functional, and people play roles in the narrative he has constructed. When someone deviates from this role, they lose all value and can be reduced to a simple physical description or a distorted memory that serves his own version of events. This view reflects his perception of human relationships as instruments of control and convenience, and his inability to tolerate any trace of independence or imperfection in others.

The madman, visibly disturbed, attempts to explain his growing concern over Kendall's behaviour.

Madman: —As for Kendall... he was completely and utterly thick.

Analyst: —That word doesn't exist.

The madman looks at him, irritated by the correction, and replies impatiently:

Madman: —Then what would you call a man who takes a photo and, ridiculously, talks to it making promises of love? For a moment, I thought our master plan had failed, and we were heading towards an absolute disaster.

The madman pauses, and on his face is a mixture of concern and resignation.

Madman: —I thought about the £1,837 Kendall had invested; practically all that was left of his family inheritance. I thought about the favours I'd called in his name, the £7 we'd spent on the Rolls, the £31 we paid for the tuxedo. —He pauses, adding with a touch of bitterness—. I thought about the lunches I had to forgo with Stingler. And let me clarify, that's a double expense, doctor, because aside from passing on the crab and the fresh orange juice from Valencia, I had to buy half a dozen eggs, boil them myself, and eat sliced bread on my own. Not to mention the tea I also paid for out of my pocket.

The madman pauses, and his tone becomes darker:

Madman: —One simply cannot afford to make such an investment without a guarantee that the plan will be carried out to the letter. And yet, there was Kendall, losing his head, throwing love promises at a mere photograph.

The analyst watches him closely, noticing that the madman is not only worried about the plan's failure, but also about the sense of betrayal he feels at Kendall's apparent change of direction. For him, every investment, every sacrifice—even the tea paid for out of his own pocket—represents a commitment to a plan that was meant to be followed without deviation. Kendall's sudden love for Nicole Cover becomes, in the madman's mind, a direct betrayal of all the effort, favours, and money invested.

The madman's speech reveals his obsession not only with the success of his plan but with absolute control over every detail and every cost. Each expense, from the Rolls to the sliced bread he had to settle for instead of crab, becomes evidence of his personal sacrifice and meticulous dedication. For the madman, these efforts were not just necessary; they were part of an implicit contract that everyone was meant to honour.

Kendall's "stupification," symbolised in his promises of love to a mere photograph, breaks this controlled structure and turns every investment into a risk of loss. The madman's obsession with the most trivial details, like the cost of his lunches or the tea he had to pay for himself, underscores his belief that the success of his plan must be guaranteed. Faced with this deviation, the madman experiences not only frustration but a sense of betrayal, seeing that the object of his manipulation has stopped obeying the logic he had designed, and instead, yielded to emotions he despises and cannot control.

The analyst, not missing a beat, reminds the madman of the outstanding debt for the bouquet of roses:

Analyst: —You forgot to mention the bouquet of 288 red roses that Lavander took to the racecourse club...

The madman smiles with a mix of irony and disdain.

Madman: —I haven't forgotten, doctor. I just still owe it. It's in poor taste to add to the balance of an operation costs you haven't even covered yet. Who knows, maybe the florists will forget about my debt. Or I could say it was Mr. Kendall who'd pay, and now that he's dead... —he shrugs indifferently—. That loss will have to be picked up by the 17 florists who gave me the roses. After all, it was midwinter, and they probably wouldn't have sold those flowers anyway.

He pauses, as if remembering another part of the plan, and continues:

Madman: —I decided someone else would take care of the "dirty work," to avoid more blunders. But, in the meantime, I had the brilliant idea of telling Mr. Kendall that his "noble relationship" with Miss Cover would... flourish. We had to keep that poor devil hooked on something.

The madman picks up his portfolio from the floor and pulls out a sepia-toned photograph of Nicole and Mr. Kendall, both smiling in a way that seems almost unreal, as if they had discovered something wonderful.

Analyst: —And who is she? —asks the analyst, noticing another photo of a slim woman with small eyes, a straight nose, and full lips, flashing a broad smile that radiates happiness.

The madman holds the photo with concealed disdain.

Madman: —She's my ex-wife... the one who was ugly and then got fat. But here, she wasn't fat yet, just ugly. —He says it with contempt, adding—. I like to keep photos of people when they look happy.

As he picks up the photos, the analyst asks a probing question:

Analyst: —So, did Nicole and Mr. Kendall really go out?

Madman: —Of course they did, doctor. After all, they were a man and a woman biologically healthy and in their reproductive years.

The madman calmly puts the photos back in his portfolio, as if this biological reality is the only reason needed to explain the attraction between Kendall and Nicole. For him, their desires and connection were merely incidental, with no other significance than fulfilling the grand scheme he had designed. In his mind, there was no room to consider the possibility of a genuine bond; only the inevitable biology and the convenience of attraction in his plans.

The madman's attitude reveals his cold, calculating perception of human relationships. For him, even gestures of affection or attraction hold no genuine value; they are mere biological accidents to be exploited or discarded as suits his plans. The way he handles the rose debt, attempting to evade responsibility, shows that he sees human emotions and connections as something he can use or ignore at his convenience.

The photo of his ex-wife, "happy" but despised, illustrates his lack of empathy and his instrumental view of people, only keeping those who are useful to him. He keeps their images not out of attachment or affection, but to remember them in a state he controls: a moment of happiness that he chooses to preserve, even if he no longer values the person themselves. This view dehumanises feelings and reduces people to "pieces" that move according to the rules he sets, underestimating any emotional depth they may experience, both Nicole and Kendall, in their real interactions.

The madman, in a somewhat reflective tone, begins to narrate how the original plan started to unravel with the unexpected bond between Kendall and Nicole Cover.

Madman: —It was at that moment, doctor, when my "days of rage" began. Nicole Cover didn't believe a word Kendall said, yet that seemed to matter little. They went to a cricket match, which, by the way, bored them both terribly. But at some point, in the midst of that tedium, they ended up kissing. And that kiss changed the dynamic between them.

The madman pauses, almost as if reliving the moment when he started to lose control over the plan.

Madman: —They left the match in the middle of a brutal snowstorm, and in the Rolls that Kendall had begun using daily since his visit to the chess salon, he drove her to her residence. Miss Cover, like a pearl slipping between his arms, let herself be carried with an utterly graceful elegance.

Analyst: —And what did you think at that moment?

Madman: —I thought I should buy the car. I couldn't keep up the façade with favours and work from mediocre clients; it wasn't profitable. Kendall and Nicole went on a trip to Manchester the following weekend, and believe me, doctor, I had to make a thousand arrangements to make sure everything went perfectly. I rented a country house that had been owned by one of my cousins and was up for sale; I even hired a couple of servants and pretended to be a frequent visitor and a friend of Mr. Kendall.

The analyst notices that the relationship between Kendall and Nicole has forced the madman to alter his plan, introducing a new dynamic he hadn't anticipated.

Madman: —Curiously, Miss Cover turned out to be useful. I had to stop calling Lavander to be Kendall's official companion to the racing events. I must admit, they made a splendid couple. Plus, Nicole had been riding horses since she was a child, and her bearing reflected that innate grace. Her sister was an exceptional rider, with an elegance that only nobility seems to bestow.

The madman falls silent for a moment, watching the analyst, who realises that the story has taken a personal turn. Nicole, someone who initially seemed a threat, had become a new pillar in the plan, replacing

UTTER CONTEMPT

Lavander and projecting the perfect image of a worthy companion for Kendall. However, for the madman, the change wasn't easy: introducing Nicole into his schemes forced him to reconsider his control over the situation and, in a way, rely on factors that were beyond his direct manipulation.

Nicole's emergence as Kendall's "official" partner reveals the madman's flexibility, who, despite his aversion to the unexpected, adapts when circumstances demand it. At first, Nicole represented a threat, someone who could dismantle his manipulations; however, upon seeing the genuine connection that developed between her and Kendall, the madman decided to adjust and capitalise on the situation. This change shows that, although obsessive and controlling, the madman understands that, at times, he can achieve his objectives by incorporating elements outside of his original design.

Furthermore, replacing Lavander with Nicole in Kendall's life not only represents a tactical adjustment but also an implicit surrender: Nicole was, in her own way, the symbol of a more authentic and natural dynamic, something Lavander, as just a "piece" in the madman's game, could never offer. Although the madman would never openly admit it, this authenticity between Kendall and Nicole forced an evolution in his methods, leading him to allow a "stone off the board" like Nicole to become a new card in his game, adapting his strategy and control to a reality that, at times, seemed to escape his grasp.

For the first time, the madman seems to show a genuine and almost reverential respect for Nicole Cover, a woman who both confuses and fascinates him at the same time.

Madman: —Nicole Cover's got an exceptional charm, doctor. I'm not sure if it's her smile or the way she squints her eyes and wrinkles her nose, completing that almost perfect face.

The analyst, sensing a different tone in his voice, watches him with genuine curiosity:

Analyst: —So, would you say Miss Cover was... pretty?

The madman, visibly startled, responds immediately, almost indignantly at the question:

Madman: —Pretty? She's truly beautiful! Perfect, a delicate piece of craftsmanship. Not even those arrogant Italian goldsmiths could make something so beautiful. Simply stunning... though, sadly, far too clever. And that combination of beauty and intelligence makes any man—especially one like me—feel a certain fear and distrust. Miss Cover, on her own, could've got those hundred million pounds without needing someone like Kendall.

The madman falls silent for a few moments, as if reflecting on the unexpected events that had altered his original plan.

Madman: —Unfortunately, love wasn't part of the deal we sealed in that old, shabby bar where I met Mr. Kendall. It's only because of that, doctor, that I can afford to criticise the relationship between my "monstrous creation" and that butterfly so perfect, so fascinating.

The analyst, sensing that the madman has trapped himself in his own game due to the very feelings he despises, asks a direct question:

Analyst: —Did you want to get rid of Miss Cover?

The madman vehemently shakes his head, as if the question were absurd:

Madman: —No, doctor, how could I get rid of my lucky charm? —He pauses, regaining his controlled tone, and continues—. Miss Cover's father is the real treasure. He dines every third day with the King and the Secretary of His Majesty, and plays bridge with the Royal House's advisers. Plus, he was a Formula cars driver in his youth. Son of a war hero, his medals aren't there by chance. Admired by all, he was the direct link to solid investment.

The madman watches the analyst, pleased to have made the strategic importance of Nicole Cover and her background clear. Nicole's presence and lineage brought with them genuine, respected influence.

UTTER CONTEMPT 75

The madman's discourse on Nicole Cover reveals an interesting ambivalence: on the one hand, he almost reverentially admires her beauty and intelligence; on the other, he sees her as a "lucky charm," a tool for his own purposes. His fear and distrust of her don't stem from rejection, but from a sense of vulnerability that someone like him, used to manipulating, rarely experiences.

The mention of Nicole's father and his connections suggests that the madman understands that Nicole's position goes far beyond her appearance or personal charm. To him, Nicole represents an invaluable opportunity to access a network of power that no favour or manipulation could guarantee on its own. His relationship with the King and the public admiration for her military lineage make her an essential link, an advantage to be protected at all costs. This blend of admiration and pragmatic calculation shows the madman in his most complex essence, torn between his genuine fascination and his cold, strategic rationality.

The madman, recalling his efforts to find the perfect gift for Nicole Cover, describes the process with a tone of satisfaction mixed with exhaustion.

Madman: —You see, doctor, if Mr. Cover's not a Lord, it's only because of his Irish origins and his refusal to accept the titles his friend, the King, has offered him. So, when I thought about a gift for his daughter, the "pearl" Nicole, I realised it had to be something absolutely unique.

The madman pauses, as if recalling the sleepless nights spent thinking of ideas for the gift.

Madman: —I spent at least six whole nights awake, turning the idea over in my head. It had to be something special, something that stood out. At first, I thought of giving her a horse, and I even considered contacting an exceptional breeder like Lord Engelton. But then I remembered Miss Cover would already have, in her personal stables, at least a dozen horses of that quality. Then I thought about commissioning an oil painting, hiring a painter from Venice or Florence to capture her beauty. But I remembered that two summers ago, a renowned French painter had already painted her.

The madman sighs, as if reliving the frustration of those days.

Madman: —Nothing seemed good enough for her, doctor. Kendall, being a mechanic, was thrilled at the idea of giving her a gift, but what could he contribute in terms of good taste? So the responsibility fell entirely on me, on my cunning.

Analyst: —So what did you decide, then?

Madman: —It wasn't an easy task. But, finally, the answer appeared before me like a flash of inspiration: a blue diamond, a "sea diamond." —The madman leans forward slightly, eyes sparkling with enthusiasm—. I contacted Mr. Karl Svelenski, a renowned jeweller, and I said, bluntly, "I need the largest blue diamond you have in your catalogue."

The analyst watches him, understanding that the madman viewed this gift as something more than a mere present; it was a symbol of the admiration and respect he, in his own way, felt for Nicole Cover. For the madman, the blue diamond represented the only jewel that could be worthy of Nicole, the only one that could express the unique value she held in his plan, and perhaps something deeper that he refused to admit.

The madman's account of choosing the perfect gift for Nicole reveals a blend of calculation and reverence. By recognising that nothing ordinary would be enough for her, the madman shows both an understanding of the complexity of her social position and a personal fascination with her. The choice of the blue diamond is not just a display of opulence; for the madman, the "sea diamond" represents something that transcends material value and reflects the perfection he himself sees in Nicole.

The symbolic value of this choice suggests that, for the madman, the gift was not only meant to impress Nicole and her circle; it had to secure his own respect and authority in the relationship between Kendall and Nicole. Although the madman does not openly admit his feelings towards her, his dedication to finding something unique and the effort invested in that detail show that Nicole represents an emotional and strategic challenge that he cannot ignore.

The analyst, intrigued, offers a chocolate to the madman and asks with interest:

Analyst: —So, you bought Miss Cover a blue diamond, did you?

The madman takes the chocolate, unwraps it slowly, and responds with satisfaction:

Madman: —Naturally, doctor. After all, it was a £100 million plan. What were a mere £15,789, the best price I got from the jeweller? When I first saw the diamond, I must admit, it was the most beautiful thing I'd ever laid eyes on. It was stunning, doctor. I examined it closely and couldn't resist leaning in to touch it.

He pauses, delighting in the memory, then adds:

Madman: —I instructed the jeweller to provide the best case and have a gold plaque engraved with the initials N.C.R. and the date 12/21. But the detail didn't stop there. I had my housekeeper purchase 350 red roses... though, of course, I told her to go to the other side of town for them, seeing as I'm still owing for that bouquet of Violet Carson roses. You know them, doctor?

The analyst, slightly surprised, nods faintly, and the madman continues with a brief description of the flowers:

Madman: —Violet Carson roses are a unique variety, a velvety red with a soft pinkish tint on the edges of each petal. They have a rich, complex fragrance, something between floral and spicy. There are no other roses that convey the same intensity and elegance. They were perfect to accompany the diamond, and so I did.

The analyst, impressed, takes in every detail, sensing a level of devotion and precision in the madman that goes beyond mere strategy. For the madman, this gift was not just an act of luxury; it was a meticulously calculated move to provoke admiration and surprise in Nicole, an emotion he saw as essential to maintaining his influence over her and her surroundings. Though the cost seemed high, to the madman it was a trivial investment compared to the guarantee of sustaining the illusion of prestige he had created.

The madman's effort to select every detail of Nicole's gift reveals his skill in blending beauty and meaning into a single expression of power. The choice of Violet Carson roses and the gold engraving were not mere ornaments; they represented an attempt to create an atmosphere of perfection and admiration around Nicole, reflecting her position and value in the madman's plan.

Each rose and the brilliant diamond symbolised his absolute control and his attempt to seduce not just Nicole, but the environment she moved in, reinforcing the image of Kendall's prestige and the madman's relevance as the true architect of that image. This display of luxury and detail expresses his view of human relationships as calculated constructs, where feelings and connections can, in his eyes, be bought or conditioned through grand gestures and carefully orchestrated moves.

The madman, with his calculated tone, explains to the analyst how each detail of Kendall's plan was carefully advancing toward a larger purpose.

Analyst: —So, was that how Mr. Kendall announced his intention to marry Miss Cover?

The madman pauses, taking the time to simplify his answer:

Madman: —Let's say it was a preamble, doctor. A logical step, I'd say. Now my client, Mr. Kendall, would be well regarded by Mr. Cover, and his daughter would be delighted with the gift. My task was simply to nudge Mr. Cover into supporting his future son-in-law in securing those £100 million. A hundred million of which, of course, his daughter would be a co-owner.

The analyst watches him closely, noticing how precisely the madman had aligned every element in the plan. The madman continues, pleased with the course of events:

Madman: —Everything was going just as I had planned. Two days before Kendall was due to visit Miss Cover to present the beautiful gift, I decided to make another important investment: I purchased a nearly new black Rolls for £27,659. It wasn't perfect or excessively ostentatious, but it was an elegant piece, freshly waxed. It was just what was needed for the gentlemanly Mr. Kendall to project the right level.

The madman relaxes a little, satisfied that every detail was in place to complete the illusion of nobility and elegance surrounding Kendall. For him, the black Rolls was not just a car; it was an extension of the image he had built of Kendall as someone worthy of Nicole's circle and, therefore, of the resources they intended to acquire. With this move, the madman had created the necessary conditions for Kendall to appear not as a simple mechanic who had risen in society, but as someone with enough sophistication and backing to be well received in the Cover family's close circle.

The madman's focus on every detail, from the diamond gift to the acquisition of the black Rolls, shows how he views the marriage between Kendall and Nicole as a strategically advantageous transaction. For him, every gesture, every investment in appearance and luxury, not only projects an image of elegance but ensures his control over the situation. The black Rolls symbolises Kendall's arrival at a status level that the madman has carefully crafted, in order to win Mr. Cover's favour and ensure the money flows as a result of that connection.

This display of strategy reveals how, for the madman, the marriage between Kendall and Nicole is not about love or genuine connection, but a calculated move in a power game. Every piece he places — from the gift to the vehicle — is meant to consolidate his influence, not only over Kendall and Nicole but over the very structure of a society in which he, though in the shadows, has constructed a narrative of wealth, prestige, and success.

The analyst, maintaining his steady tone, takes a bottle of liquor from the sideboard next to the desk and addresses the madman:

Analyst: —Two ice cubes, right?

The madman looks at him, somewhat puzzled, trying to decipher the intention behind the offer:

Madman: —Is it real?

The analyst nods, and with golden tongs, places two ice cubes in an old-fashioned glass. Finally, the madman accepts the drink, extends his arm, and sips slowly while the analyst watches him in silence. After a pause, the analyst speaks again:

Analyst: —So, were Nicole and Mr. Kendall about to marry?

The madman nods with a slight sigh, as if remembering the days before everything started to unravel.

Madman: —That was the plan, doctor. But, as often happens, the devil arrives, and everything falls apart. However, before everything changed, Mr. Cover really did help us. I managed to get him to commit some of his contacts in Parliament to invest in an oil well project in Texas, on the Kendall family's property.

Madman: *He pauses and continues, his voice now tinged with a slight satisfaction.*

Madman: —The meeting with Mr. Cover was a perfect spectacle, two days before Nicole received the "sea diamond." That afternoon was like a dream, doctor. Inspired by the tale of my maternal great-grandfather, who kidnapped my great-grandmother from a convent on the mainland, I decided to hire a hot-air balloon so that the happy couple could float through the air.

Analyst: —A hot-air balloon? —he asks, a mix of astonishment and disbelief.

Madman: —That's right. A flight among the clouds, full of sweet words and kisses, to seal the deal. *The madman smiles.* While they were up in the air, doctor, I did what I do best: I negotiated with the bride's father on the conditions for securing his support. It was the perfect opportunity to gain the backing of this distinguished man and his friends from Parliament. The sum my esteemed son-in-law desired was finally within reach.

The madman falls silent, savouring the memory of that perfectly executed strategy, while the analyst watches, realising how every element of this "dream" was meant to solidify a single objective: Cover's support and his influence in Parliament. For the madman, the balloon flight wasn't just a romantic gesture for the couple; it was a calculated move to seal a crucial deal, capitalising on the air of promise and commitment.

The madman's tale of the hot-air balloon flight and his meeting with Mr. Cover reveals his skill in using theatrics and emotional manipulation as negotiation tools. For him, every detail—the "sea diamond," the flight among the clouds—was carefully crafted to reinforce the image of a perfect commitment, while he privately negotiated with the bride's father.

The story of his great-grandfather, adding a touch of romance and adventure, not only highlights his love for dramatic narratives but also symbolises his ability to manipulate emotions and create moments that distract others, nudging them to accept his terms. The flight among the clouds becomes a metaphor for how the madman leads others to "dream," while he maintains control over the transactions. Thus, the marriage between Kendall and Nicole, which might seem like a union based on love and prestige, is ultimately a calculated negotiation, where the madman uses love and romance as just another resource in his strategy to reach the coveted sum.

The madman, evidently relishing the details of his own preparation, recounts to the analyst how each element of his appearance and behaviour was meticulously planned.

Madman: —The next day, doctor, I made my way to the Cover residence in Nothing Hill. And believe me, every detail was carefully thought out. For the occasion, I decided to forge a couple of decorations to present myself as a war hero. I wore my finest watch and that black tailcoat with striped grey trousers I reserve for very special occasions. The handmade Italian shirt was starched three times at the collar and three times at each cuff; nothing was left to chance. The Italian shoes, made of fine goatskin, and a pigskin-lined briefcase completed my outfit, giving me an air of aristocracy that even my mother wouldn't question.

The analyst listens, fascinated, while the madman continues, almost reverently, regarding the details of his attire.

Madman: —To unwind a bit, I first went to the chess room and accepted the "generosity" of my esteemed Sir William Stingler. I had my usual lunch: fresh crab, but this time I decided to accompany it with French champagne. You know, doctor, the one they say is "like drinking stars." But in my case, I think I was drinking diamonds.

Analyst: —And how did Sir William take it?

Madman: —I took out my wallet and, to everyone's surprise, endorsed a cheque to the Chess Club. The waiter and Sir William himself raised their eyebrows as if they had witnessed something forbidden. I insisted it was nothing to worry about, but you know how those people are: they love to "hurt" with their disdain and that collection of petty phrases.

The madman pauses, recalling the impact he left in the room.

Madman: —I bid them farewell with a procession worthy of a head of state, stepping into the beautifully waxed Rolls. I set my Swiss watch to the reception clock, doctor, because I thought it might be the last time I'd be in that place and with those people.

The analyst observes, sensing the symbolism in each step the madman took, almost as if it were a farewell to a world he considered inferior.

Analyst: —And the meeting, what happened after that? Where did you go, and who was there?

The madman looks at him, a smile of intrigue forming.

Madman: —Ah, doctor, the meeting... I arrived at the Cover residence with the dignity a head of state would bring to a royal audience. *He pauses, savouring the anticipation.* Since we're on a roll, let me tell you that... upon entering, I was greeted by a butler who could well have been a retired general. The room, tastefully decorated, was like a museum of lineage and power, and there, waiting for me, was Mr. Cover... and someone else.

The analyst, intrigued, senses that every detail was calculated to impress Mr. Cover and consolidate the support the madman was desperate to gain. For the madman, this visit wasn't just a business meeting; it was the culmination of a carefully choreographed sequence, where each move and accessory was designed to reinforce the image of prestige and power he had crafted for himself and for Kendall.

The madman's meticulous preparation for the meeting reflects his obsession with appearance and the impact it can have on those around him. Every detail, from the Italian shirt to the forged decorations, becomes a symbol of power and authority that he himself has fabricated. For the madman, these insignias aren't just ornaments; they're a mask that grants him the respect and status he needs to manipulate his surroundings.

The lunch in the chess room, with the unexpected cheque gesture, underscores his ability to create a dramatic and final impression. The farewell at the club symbolises the closing of a chapter in his life and a kind of "rise" to a realm of greater power and opportunity, represented by the meeting at the Cover residence. For the madman, each step and every detail forms part of a carefully woven narrative, a story in which he controls how he will be seen and the effect he will leave on those around him, always in line with his strategic ambitions.

The madman, with his voice laced with satisfaction, continues to describe his triumphant entrance into the Cover residence, capturing every detail of that crucial encounter.

Madman: —As I entered, I greeted Mr. Cover with a brief, almost imperceptible bow. It was a minimal gesture, doctor, which he returned in kind. The butler, in his impeccable formality, asked me to announce my name. *The madman pauses, relishing the memory.* Never, doctor, *never* had I pronounced my name with such pride. It echoed through the room, as though it were a title in itself.

The analyst listens, fascinated, as the madman recreates the scene with enthusiasm.

Madman: —I advanced with elegant steps, not counting them. I must have imagined that scene thousands, perhaps hundreds of thousands of times in my life. As I reached my place, thirteen elegantly dressed gentlemen stood up and bowed their heads, welcoming me, doctor. Without a word, I understood they wished for me to sit and share their company.

The madman smiles, almost savouring each name he pronounces.

Madman: —I drank a scotch as they introduced me: Lord Walterford here, Sir Adam Strussbert there... names with a resonance and weight, each one more grandiose than the last. Finally, Mr. Cover introduced me as the general administrator of the Kendall family's assets.

This version carries the tone of a Londoner with slightly formal but still relatable expressions, focusing on elegance and dramatic flair.

Analyst: —So then?

Madman: —Well, doctor, it was my time to shine. From my portfolio, I pulled out a bundle of documents, carefully sealed and stamped, yet visible enough to make a good impression without overdoing it. Among them, I spread out the map of a 45,000-acre estate in Texas. Yes, doctor, all the way across the world, but at that moment, it was like a distant, tempting jewel before them.

The madman looks at the analyst with an intense expression, as though still feeling the weight of those men's stares.

Madman: —I addressed them firmly: "Gentlemen! As you well know, my client, Mr. Kendall, from a distinguished family, owns a prosperous estate in the American territory, in the state of Texas. And on that estate, gentlemen, lies an oil deposit, the black gold that will propel the world for…" —and here I paused, deliberately, doctor, because one must know when to speculate—"one hundred years… or maybe a thousand." Who knows, but we all know that oil will keep driving us, as it has in recent decades.

The madman smiles, pleased with the effect of his words.

Madman: —My words echoed in their ears, doctor, each one carefully crafted to stir their greed and sense of opportunity. Then, among them, a tall, thin man, like a walking stick, stood up. It was old Standish. "I know Mr. Kendall, a chess genius, exceedingly clever," he said. And, without further ado, he declared that he would invest thirty million pounds from his clients' funds, and five million from his own pocket.

The analyst, taken aback by the scale of the offer, fills the madman's glass as he asks incredulously:

Analyst: —Did Standish really say this without you paying him a penny?

The madman accepts the glass, a triumphant smile on his lips.

Madman: —That's right, doctor. I didn't pay him a penny. Sometimes, money isn't needed when you know how to create the perfect image. At that moment, I knew I had triumphed… as only the greats triumph.

The analyst watches the madman, realising that for him, the victory didn't lie in the sum promised by Standish, but in his ability to manipulate the perceptions of those present. The meeting wasn't just a business deal; it was the result of a choreography executed with precision, where every gesture and word from the madman was designed to project an image of unbeatable authority and prestige. In the end, Standish's willingness to invest without question reflected, for the madman, the greatest success: the power to control the minds and desires of the London elite without the need for bribes, simply by manipulating the context and environment in his favour.

The madman's presentation at the Cover residence reveals how every movement and word of his was intentional, not just to generate interest in the project but to establish an image of influence and power that he had meticulously crafted. The dramatic pause in his speech and the reference to the "fortune" in Texas show his skill at weaving a narrative of imminent prosperity, appealing to the greed and sense of belonging of those present.

Standish's commitment to invest millions, without receiving any incentive, validates the madman's success not just in financial terms but in his ability to project an impenetrable and seductive image. For the madman, this moment of public acceptance becomes the true reward, the culmination of his absolute control over the perception and desires of those around him, and a symbol of his final triumph in the world of appearances he himself had constructed.

The madman, with a tone of satisfaction and a slight touch of euphoria, recounts to the analyst how the compliments and promises at the meeting culminated in an unexpected victory.

Madman: —As was only natural, the first thing I did was congratulate Mr. Standish. Not only did I express my gratitude, but I also made him aware of his superior intelligence and vision of the energy landscape. After him, two other distinguished gentlemen spoke, commenting that they had seen Mr. Kendall at the opera with a lady of exceptional refinement, and that, without a doubt, he had conquered the most beautiful woman in London.

Analyst: —And you...?

Madman: —Ah, doctor, I subtly corrected them. I stated that Miss Cover was not only the most beautiful in London but in the entire Isle, and perhaps the entire planet. —He pauses, savouring the memory—. Upon hearing this, Mr. Cover puffed up with pride and, believe me, doctor, I saw his eyes fill with tears that he tried to hide. He took a deep breath and, as if sealing a fate, declared that he would support his "son-in-law's" request. He called Kendall son-in-law, can you believe it? At that moment, doctor, Mr. Kendall gained, for me, a hint of respect. I even felt like a godfather, or something of the sort.

The analyst nods, understanding the blend of cynicism and sincerity in the madman's words, who seemed to relish the effect of his manipulations as much as the financial success itself.

Madman: —In about 37 minutes, at that table, futures contracts were signed worth a total of 157 million pounds. The room was filled with toasts and congratulations, doctor, and every man in the room congratulated himself on his "intelligence" and "generosity."

Analyst: —And you? What did you do?

Madman: —I had another scotch, naturally, and carefully filed away each signed contract. I made sure that a correspondent in my service would carry out all the necessary arrangements to ensure the money was collected within the next 96 hours, as is our custom. The atmosphere was a real spectacle of egos, doctor, each one congratulating himself for his cleverness.

The analyst listens intently, realising that for the madman, this last toast and the confirmation of investments not only represented a financial triumph but the climax of a series of manipulations executed with precision. For the madman, there was no greater victory than seeing these men, convinced of their "intelligence," securing the fortune he had planned to obtain from the very start.

The madman's account of the compliments, toasts, and signed contracts shows how the meeting became a celebration of egos, where every participant saw themselves as part of a visionary elite. The madman's subtle correction, elevating Nicole Cover from "the most beautiful in London" to "the most beautiful in the entire planet," demonstrates his skill at playing with the emotions and personal pride of those present, provoking an immediate and deep response from Mr. Cover.

For the madman, the true reward was not in the money, but in the confirmation of his influence. The willingness of the gentlemen to see him, and Kendall, as figures of authority and prestige represents the pinnacle of his success. The final meeting becomes a symbol of his ability to create an alternative reality, where his manipulations and narratives made each participant feel intelligent and generous.

The madman continues his tale, describing with enthusiasm the climax of his success and the sudden arrival of justice the next morning.

Madman: —That night, doctor, after the meeting at the Cover residence, I ordered the chauffeur to take me around London in the Rolls. For over two hours, we drove through the city; I was so ecstatic about my success that I wanted to savour every moment. Finally, I arrived at the apartment I shared with Mr. Kendall. The news of his success had already reached him, no need for me to tell him. I congratulated him with a hearty hug, and he, naturally, expected us to have a toast together. But I, doctor, was more exhausted than I had ever been in my life.

He pauses, as if still feeling the weight of that exhaustion.

Madman: —I decided it was time for a change. Carefully hung up each garment, slipped into my slippers, and lay down in bed. I nodded off instantly, and dreamt I was floating in a hot air balloon with the fine gents who'd joined our company as partners, and they were asking me to steer the contraption like some modern-day Jason leading the Argonauts to new horizons. It was a restful dream, even though it didn't last long.

The analyst listens attentively, picking up on the strange mix of euphoria and exhaustion in the madman's voice.

Madman: —At precisely 7:06 on the morning of the 20th of December, reality came crashing in. A constable, with four chaps from

Scotland Yard in tow, waltzed into my home. They were there over some allegation from Miss Stephany McBride, accusing Mr Kendall and myself of fraud, swindling, and a smattering of minor charges I can't quite recall. Right away, they confiscated everything: my typewriter—still in pristine condition—and my library of 16,601 books, originals and some rather fine Greek forgeries, which the inspectors, amusingly, took as the genuine article.

Analyst: —And what about the diamond?

Madman: —Ah yes, the 14-carat blue diamond, legitimate and lawfully purchased, as Chief Inspector would later confirm. They also seized my four pairs of Italian leather shoes, top-quality; two Swiss watches, four French fountain pens, and a pigskin briefcase in black. Inside the case were various documents they intended to check for authenticity.

Analyst: —What happened next?

Madman: —They informed Mr Kendall and me that we were to accompany them to the Scotland Yard building. But, Doctor, I'd anticipated as much. The night before, I'd seen my neighbour Joseph Garland's lad, about fourteen, and instructed him to collect, in my name, from all the gents listed on the last thirteen pages of my address book. Lucky for me, I'd left it with him that evening. Garland's a sharp lad, clever enough to get the funds together before the coppers had even spread their doom about town.

The madman pauses, and the analyst watches him, spellbound by the calm with which he lays out his contingency plan.

Madman: —So really, all I had to ask for was verification of the legal purchase of the "Sea Diamond." Paid for it with my personal account at Barclays; no crime in buying a trinket for a lovely woman, I explained, cool as a cucumber, to the chief inspector.

Analyst: —And what did he say? —asks the analyst, barely containing his curiosity.

The madman smiles, as if savouring the memory of the moment.

Madman: —The chief inspector fixed me with a stare, as if he was trying to see through every word of mine. Didn't answer right off. Just said, "We'll verify your account and every one of your purchases, sir. Don't worry." Then he asked me to accompany him to Scotland Yard.

The analyst watches the madman, who exudes a wry calm, as if even in the worst of moments he has an answer for every question and a plan for every curveball. For him, this police intervention was merely a minor hurdle, a foreseen obstacle, with preparations laid out well in advance. He knew the money would keep flowing thanks to Garland, and that the seizure of luxury items and documents was just a temporary inconvenience. Everything, in his mind, was firmly under control.

The madman's account of the Scotland Yard operation reveals how he remains serene and confident in his ability to solve any predicament, even in a crisis. By delegating the task of collecting his contacts' dues to young Garland, he displays foresight and a deep understanding of the importance of keeping the cash flow steady. The ease with which he justifies the diamond's purchase, in the face of fraud allegations, shows his knack for projecting innocence and impeccable character, even when evidence might suggest otherwise.

To the madman, the police intervention was just another challenge in his game of manipulation, another situation to overcome to maintain the narrative of success and power he's carefully crafted. Garland's readiness to collect the funds and the confident manner in which he recounts the procedure to the inspector attest to his obsession with absolute control over every aspect of his life, including unforeseen events. This calculated calm reinforces his conviction that, no matter the situation, he'll always find a way out, relying on his ability to shape others' perceptions and his contingency plans, which highlight his skill at anticipating every move.

The madman continues his tale, detailing how, despite Scotland Yard's intervention, he managed to retain control of the situation and his plans to come through unscathed.

Madman: —In the end, they confirmed I had indeed lawfully purchased the Sea Diamond using my life savings. The jeweller, in fact, was quite insulted that my good name—and my "friend" and partner Mr Kendall's—had been called into question. The chief inspector, at my request, returned the jewel without delay.

The madman smiles, relishing every detail, and continues:

Madman: —I explained to the chief inspector that I could account for every accusation Miss McBride had levelled against myself and "my business partner." However, Doctor, upon hearing me out, the inspector fixed me with a gloomy expression and said, "Then, you'll be staying. He"—gesturing to Mr Kendall— "may leave. I'd simply ask him not to leave the city."

Analyst: —And how did Kendall react?

Madman: —Kendall looked at me with gratitude. Doctor, no one's ever looked at me like that. I instructed him to head over to Cover House and keep his cool. If anyone asked about the police, he was to say that I was resolving a matter with an old associate who'd made a mistake. Kendall took the diamond with him and even promised to speed up its delivery. What's more, Doctor, he assured me he'd send over a decent solicitor.

The analyst listens, fascinated by the strategic calm the madman exhibits even in the stickiest of situations.

Madman: —I watched him leave, and at that moment, I knew I had a bit of time. If Scotland Yard chose to grill me on my bogus war medals, I'd have a riposte: I'd say that Napoleon crowned himself emperor without ever being a general. As for the Texas documents, it would take at least six days to get a response. Given that it was noon on a Friday, I had ample time to sort my way out.

Analyst: —What was the plan?

Madman: —My alibi was flawless. I'd planned to ask for leave to visit my ex-wife, the one who was plain to start with and only grew stouter with time. I'd beg her to take me in at her... pigsty, full of cows and hogs. From there, I'd buy myself a ticket to the Mediterranean.

He pauses and then continues:

Madman: —However, a phone call changed everything. It was perplexing, Doctor, but it brought me back to my senses and made me ditch the absurd idea of hiding out on a farm. In the end, my disdain for that woman and her pigsty runs too deep.

The analyst watches him, realising the madman had toyed with a desperate escape plan, but that something in that call brought him back to his usual mindset of control and sophistication. Despite the mounting pressure, he still trusted his ability to manipulate every element in his favour. To him, hiding at his ex-wife's was merely a distracting detail in a far more elaborate contingency plan, where each move had been designed to preserve his dignity and standing.

The madman's narration of his exchange with the inspector and his escape plan reveals his skill at staying cool and collected, even in the tensest situations. By preparing a story about his bogus war medals and predicting the response time for the Texas documents, he shows the foresight and precision of a man who knows how to work within the grey areas of the law. The phone call, which restores his "sanity," shows how his mind quickly resets to his original plans, abandoning the undignified idea of seeking refuge in a place he finds humiliating.

His disdain for his ex-wife and her "pigsty" symbolises his utter rejection of any escape that doesn't preserve his image of power and control. To him, his dignity and how he's seen by society are so paramount that he'd rather face the charges in his own world than take refuge somewhere he sees as a personal defeat. This mindset underscores his obsession with status and appearance, guiding him to decisions always aimed at safeguarding his pride and the image of power he's spent years crafting.

The analyst, intrigued, can't resist taking a sip of his coffee while he listens to every word from the madman, whose unruffled composure holds steady throughout his tale.

Analyst: —Who called, and what for?

Madman: —It was Mr Standish, Doctor —he answered with calculated calm—. Calling to confirm the property in Texas, which he'd discovered belonged to a certain Josephine Kendall, apparently no direct relation to Mr Kendall. Turned out the property spanned 47,500 acres, not the 45,000 I'd stated, and the taxes hadn't been paid in years. Even so, Standish didn't hesitate to assure me he'd entrusted his family's savings to me.

The analyst blinks, processing the irony of the situation:

Analyst: —And Josephine… wasn't related to Kendall?

Madman: —Exactly, Doctor, the ultimate irony. Standish thought his savings were safe in Kendall's hands and in that property. Fate had played right into my hands, and there wasn't any real crime to pursue. A few minutes later, a man in a sober suit entered Scotland Yard and introduced himself as Sir Gordon Stanton, solicitor to the Cover family. He assured me he'd get me out of there. I, with an air of superiority, confirmed that I was already on my way out, that it was all a misunderstanding, and, at most, a 'bit of a fuss over a lady.' Sir Gordon shrugged and left as swiftly as he'd arrived.

The analyst watches the madman, who continues recounting each step with an almost unshakeable calm, explaining how he'd navigated every obstacle with the same ease with which he'd manipulated his surroundings.

Madman: —Finally, the Chief Inspector told me not to leave London but said that, for now, given the circumstances, I was free to go. So, I left, Doctor. And on returning to my flat, there was young Garland, waiting for me with a shoebox. He handed it over, and as I opened it, I saw it was packed with banknotes of all denominations. He confirmed that he'd collected the lot.

Analyst: —And what did you do?

Madman: —We sat together at the empty table in the flat and began counting, note by note. —The madman pauses, a faint smile playing on his lips—. In that moment, Doctor, I felt as though I'd won a significant game, perhaps the most significant of all.

The analyst observes the madman's calm and senses that, for him, counting that money wasn't merely a check on his success; it was a way of savouring each step in a strategy that had played out exactly as planned. The cash in the shoebox, far from being just a material resource, was a tangible symbol of his ability to manipulate, deceive, and outwit anyone—from his associates to the police itself. Every note represented a piece in the complex puzzle of lies and machinations he'd built, and the fact that the system couldn't find any genuine crime only strengthened, in his mind, his absolute mastery over the situation.

The madman's account of how he'd escaped Scotland Yard, thanks to Standish's intervention and the solicitor Sir Gordon, reveals how he'd planned his exit with the same precision as the rest of his scheme. Fate, according to him, seemed to favour his side, turning each setback into an opportunity to reaffirm his control and cunning. Garland's readiness to gather the funds and the speed with which he amassed the money shows that, even in moments of apparent weakness, the madman maintained complete control over every aspect of his life.

The shoebox full of money symbolises the culmination of his success in the game of appearances and manipulation. Counting the cash on his empty table reinforces the sense of victory and control he'd managed to construct in his environment, representing not only the fruition of his plans but a tangible proof of his ability to twist even the justice system to his will. In the madman's world, the lack of sufficient evidence not only absolves him but reinforces his belief that, above rules and laws, lies his intelligence and skill in shaping reality to his own ends.

The madman, with his ever-calculated tone, goes on detailing the events after his release and the bond he'd formed with Garland.

Analyst: —And then what? What did you do with the money and that boy? —asks the analyst, a mix of intrigue and eagerness to know the outcome.

Madman: —Well, Doctor, naturally, I decided to celebrate. We went out to buy something to eat and toasted with a couple of glasses—nothing too strong. I began calling him 'Mr Garland,' and he, with that youthful spontaneity, named me 'Lord.' An undeserved title, surely, but one I accepted from my new associate with pleasure. You never know, Doctor; that scruffy lad might one day end up King of England... with a little guidance from me.

The madman smiles, as if he genuinely believes in his ability to shape Garland's destiny. He continues his story with a calmness that contrasts with the analyst's increasing urgency to hear more.

Madman: —Then, I decided to take him to Stanford's tailor shop, just a couple of streets from my flat. I asked the tailor to show us his finest shirts, though, unfortunately, none were Italian or handmade. But they were decent enough, and as the Kendall family's property manager, I bought one for myself and another for Mr Garland. What's more, Doctor: we found two suits that fit us perfectly, one in grey and the other in brown. I took the liberty of acquiring a top hat for myself and a fine tie for Mr Garland—not silk, but it looked quite dapper.

Analyst: —And what else did you do?

Madman: —We donned our new clothes immediately. Though my Rolls hadn't yet been returned, I asked our driver, Jason Miller, to contact a friend of mine to hire the finest car available. Half an hour later, the vehicle was ready. We then headed to the Cover residence.

The madman pauses, and the analyst watches him, noting how each detail of the visit had been meticulously planned to maintain his image of prestige.

Madman: —Upon arrival, the butler announced me, and we were welcomed into a small gathering where the company's associates appeared enthusiastic. As I understood it, Mr Kendall had explained that Miss Stephany McBride's claim against me was merely a 'professional matter' and that Scotland Yard hadn't found anything of note. So, Doctor, when they saw me enter, the cheerfulness was overwhelming. Mr Cover, with a wide grin, took me by the arm and whispered, "Nicole and her associate have left, but I think tonight we'll make an important announcement."

Analyst: —And you?

Madman: "Upon hearing those words, I decided to take precautions. I asked Mr Garland to go with the driver to a warehouse and buy 24 bottles of French champagne. I was confident that all it required was patience, doctor. In my mind, the situation was fully under control."

The analyst observes the madman, fascinated by the calm and control he radiates, even in situations that would be chaotic for most. His relationship with Garland and the preparations for the meeting at Cover's residence weren't mere trivialities; they were part of the madman's strategy to solidify his position and project an image of confidence and prestige. Every decision, from the suit to the champagne, was directed at strengthening his position, maintaining the illusion of success and absolute control.

The relationship he describes with Garland reveals his knack for identifying unexpected allies and shaping them to suit his own ends. By addressing Garland as "Mr" and accepting the title of "Lord" from him, the madman creates a dynamic of loyalty that reinforces his hold over the young man, keeping him as an associate ready to follow his lead.

The visit to Cover's residence, preceded by meticulous attention to his appearance and the order for champagne, demonstrates how the madman leaves nothing to chance when it comes to his image and influence. The willingness of partners and the backing of Cover ensure that his position remains solid, despite McBride's accusations or investigations by Scotland Yard. Every gesture and detail, from the tailoring to the luxury car, reflects his obsession with prestige and control—a formula that, to him, spells success in a world of appearances and power.

The madman continues his tale, his tone a blend of disbelief and despair, as the analyst watches silently, capturing each emotion.

Madman: "Minutes later, doctor, the enormous door of Cover's residence swung open, and Miss Nicole appeared alone, dissolved in uncontrollable tears. Seeing her, I felt my world slipping away. I ran towards her, desperate. My mind was flooded with disjointed images: I thought of a wolf, a weasel... I shook my head like a hunter scanning the horizon for ducks. But I couldn't see Kendall."

Analyst: "And what did you do then?"

Madman: "I gently cupped Nicole's face in my hands and whispered to her, 'What's happened, where is Kendall?' She looked at me with her hazel eyes, filled with tears, and said, 'He's dead!'"

The analyst listens attentively, watching as the madman delves into the memory of that heart-wrenching moment.

Madman: "I couldn't understand, doctor. I felt the air drain out of me, and before I knew it, I was doubled over, clutching my knees. It was as if a hammer had struck my chest. I stammered, 'How? What's happened?' In my mind, I thought of an accident... maybe a lightning strike, or a hunter's stray shot."

He pauses, then continues, as though the memory still shakes him.

Madman: "And then, through sobs, she confessed: 'It was me.' At that moment, doctor, it felt impossible. How could a creature so beautiful commit such an atrocity? 'I don't understand...' I murmured, as her father held her and she wept inconsolably."

Analyst: "What did she say to you?"

Madman: "In a broken voice, Nicole said, 'It was just a game... a tasteless joke.' Dressed like a fairy tale sprite, doctor, she explained through tears, 'I told him I'd first thought he was a mechanic, someone clumsy, brutish, beautifully stupid.' And upon hearing those words, Kendall ran, threw himself off the bridge over the old ravine, and struck his head."

The madman falls silent, as though he still struggles to comprehend it. Then he continues, in a sombre tone.

Madman: "Without a second thought, I left the residence, accompanied by a few men carrying torches. Nicole was screaming in the distance, 'He's dead, dead!'"

The analyst watches in silence, sensing the blend of pain and confusion in the madman. For him, Nicole's confession and Kendall's tragic death represent a crack in his carefully crafted world, a tragedy that shakes the foundations of his strategy and manipulations. In his hands, he had success and the approval of the elite, but Kendall's death seems to have abruptly torn away that victory, plunging him into a reality where his control over events crumbles.

Nicole's confession and Kendall's suicide reveal the fragility of the reality the madman constructed, where his manipulations and façades proved insufficient to withstand the unpredictability of human emotions. Nicole's reaction, unwittingly triggering the tragedy, shows how even in a world controlled by the madman, people act according to their own impulses, beyond the narratives he imposes.

For the madman, Kendall's death is more than a personal loss or a setback in his plan; it is proof that, no matter how much he tries to shape people and manipulate situations, there are aspects of human nature he cannot control. This moment, marked by helplessness and bewilderment, symbolises the limits of his power and the shattering of the illusion of invulnerability he had maintained until then.

With a tone of irony mixed with darkness, the madman continues his story, detailing the moments following Kendall's death.

Madman: "When I reached the old ravine, I saw his bloodied body, and I knew, doctor, that Nicole Cover was right. Her scorn had destroyed him. The family physician, Sir Alex Vitton, confirmed the news. The police were called immediately, but Mr. Cover wasn't about to let them take his daughter, and I... well, I'd lost my associate, Stephany McBride, and now Mr Kendall."

He pauses, as if still coming to terms with the inevitability of that decision.

Madman: "I took a deep breath, and we agreed to report it as an accident. People, after all, stumble, fall, hit their heads... and die. That's how we presented it to the police: a simple accident. Doctor, I wouldn't have killed Mr Kendall."

The analyst listens intently, as the madman adds, in an almost ironic tone:

Madman: "Life's little ironies, I suppose; today I'm the administrator of Cover-Kendall Oil and Mining. The oilfield on those 47,500 acres is as real as you and I. And as for Mr Garland... he's now an oil and gas specialist, turned into a respectable businessman."

Analyst: "And the case? Was it closed?"

Madman: "Not entirely, doctor. The prosecutor reopened the case, stating that there wasn't enough evidence to conclude Kendall's death was accidental. But, if I may offer a bit of advice, should you be filling in the report... —" the madman fixes him with a steady gaze— "I'd suggest you write that he was killed by sheer, utter contempt."

The analyst observes the madman, struck by the candour of that last statement. For the madman, Kendall's death wasn't the result of a mere accident, but the consequence of something far darker and more profound: the devastating power of scorn. In his mind, Nicole's disdain for Kendall not only drove him to despair but pushed him over the edge to his death. To the madman, that's the real cause, the one that will remain invisible in any official report, but which he understands as the true reason behind the tragedy.

The madman's account of the Kendall case's resolution reveals his view of the tragedy as an inevitable result of disdain. The way he and

Cover agreed to present Kendall's death as an accident illustrates an attempt to protect the image and interests of those involved, though the madman seems to acknowledge with a touch of cynicism the falsehood of that story. The irony of his rise as administrator of Cover-Kendall and young Garland's success reinforces his conviction that, ultimately, contempt is the hidden force behind everything: it can not only destroy lives but also reorder power and relationships around those who wield it.

The madman's final suggestion to list "sheer, utter contempt" as the cause of death is his way of highlighting the insidious power that, in his view, can affect people more profoundly than any physical blow. In this sense, scorn is not merely an emotion or attitude but a weapon capable of causing irreversible changes in people's lives, regardless of their status or intelligence.

The End